John Esten Cooke, Anas Todkill

My lady Pokahontas

A true relation of Virginia, writ by Anas Todkill, Puritan and pilgrim

John Esten Cooke, Anas Todkill

My lady Pokahontas

A true relation of Virginia, writ by Anas Todkill, Puritan and pilgrim

ISBN/EAN: 9783743305816

Manufactured in Europe, USA, Canada, Australia, Japa

Cover: Foto ©Raphael Reischuk / pixelio.de

Manufactured and distributed by brebook publishing software
(www.brebook.com)

John Esten Cooke, Anas Todkill

My lady Pokahontas

My Lady Pokahontas

A TRUE RELATION OF VIRGINIA. WRIT
BY ANAS TODKILL, PURITAN
AND PILGRIM

With Notes by

JOHN ESTEN COOKE

BOSTON
HOUGHTON, MIFFLIN AND COMPANY
New York: 11 East Seventeenth Street
The Riverside Press, Cambridge
1885

The Riverside Press, Cambridge:
Electrotyped and Printed by H. O. Houghton & Co.

PREFACE.

ANAS TODKILL was a brave and trusty sol- *dier of the first Virginia years: adhered to Smith in all his struggles with the factions at Jamestown: took part in the fierce combats with the Indians on the York and Rappahannock: and his name is signed to a number of the old "relations" as both actor and author.*

As to the writer's personality, the present MS. leaves nothing in doubt; and as to the credibility of his historic statements, the notes will show that these are often minutely corroborated by the great original American authority, the "Generall Historie of Virginia, New England, and the Summer Isles."

Even in the pages which relate to the love romance of two celebrated personages, — to the joys and sorrows, the passionate longings and regrets, which made up their lives, — the worthy "Puritan and Pilgrim" seems only to give the details of events and incidents briefly indicated in the contemporary chronicles.

TABLE OF CONTENTS.

PAGE

I. Unworthy Anas Todkill, Puritan, his Early Years . 1

II. I talk with Captain Smith and Master Shakespeare at the Mermaid 5

III. I go on the Virginia Voyage, and what followed at Jamestown 16

IV. My Captain tells how an Angel saved Him 25

V. How I first see my Lady Pokahontas 32

VI. The Strange Antics of Pokahontas 36

VII. Of God's Mercy to his Unworthy Servant through the Blessed Pokahontas 45

VIII. How my Captain loveth the Child of a Cursed Generation 54

IX. Hawks and Cormorants (so I call Such) 62

X. I go once more with my Captain to the Place of Retreat 70

XI. We lose him whose Loss was our Deaths 75

XII. How Master Ratcliffe was a Dead Corpse on the York River 81

XIII. We go through the Wilderness to the Land of Canaan 88

XIV. How Some One did break a Poor Man on the Wheel . 94

XV. How my Lady Pokahontas is brought to Jamestown a Prisoner 101

XVI. I make Acquaintance of Master Rolfe 107

XVII. I think, Sure 't is better to be off with the Old Love ere on with the New 115

XVIII. *We sail up York River with my Lady, and what followeth* *120*

XIX. *How my Lady Pokahontas asketh, — Must she ?* . . *130*

XX. *My Lady leaneth on a Tree and weepeth* *137*

XXI. *Of the City of Henricus and my Lady's Little Divell that was made a Christian* *140*

XXII. *Of the Trick the High Marshal would play on the Emperor, but he would not* *150*

XXIII. *My Lady goes to England* *156*

XXIV. *I go to the Globe Theatre* *162*

XXV. *And meet again with Captain Smith and Master Shakespeare* *167*

XXVI. *How Smith telleth he was not dead, and crieth, " O Heaven! could she not wait ?"* *175*

XXVII. *Of the Valiant Captain Smith's Last Greeting with my Lady Pokahontas* *179*

XXVIII. *How my Lady Pokahontas passed in Peace* . . . *188*

My Lady Pokahontas

I.

Unworthy Anas Todkill, Puritan, his Early Years.

HEN that blessed damozel, my dear Lady Pokahontas, died untimely, I fell into a great wonder at the mysterious ways of Providence that put out that bright light of our time so sudden. Virginia had much need of her to bring her people to the knowledge of our Saviour. But she went away to heaven even at the moment when she was returning to her country, and her hope to have builded up a New Jerusalem in that Heathennesse had no fruit, but was buried in her grave. She had surely done her work to God's honour and immortal glory; natheless, ne'er was it begun. A pilgrim and stranger, she was called to the Land of Peace. When about

How my Lady passed in peace.

I serve in Transylvania.

to set forth with her babe on the Virginia voyage, she goes on that other, from which none comes back. Sure her dear and blessed hands had overturned the Divell's kingdom there ; but she is gone, and the frame of that great business is fall'n into her tomb.

How it chanced that I, the Puritan Anas Todkill, came to love her, this true relation showeth the reader. 'T is but little I need say of my life before the Virginia adventure, wherein I saw what Master Drayton calleth "Earth's only Paradise." All the Todkills, methinks, from the beginning of the world have been Puritans ; and this Anas sees the light for the first time in Kent, England, and grows to boyhood, and learns to read, and a thirst seizes him to see the world. So he steals away from home and wanders off to the Flanders wars ; thence he goes and takes part in the fierce battles of Transylvania, where Duke Sigismund is fighting the murtherous Turks. My captain was that dear and loyal soldier, John Smith, who was knighted by the Prince for slaying three Turkish champions in single combat, and, under that chevalier, we oft conquered. But the evil day came, as it comes at last to all.

At the bloody and dismal fight of the Ro- *Back in Kent.* ther Thurm fortune changed. The Christians did their part, and left their bodies in testimony of their minds; but the Turks overcame us, and I was cut down and lay past all sense and remembrance.

That I lived was due to Smith, who dragged me out, and so I escaped; he himself was taken prisoner and sold to slavery, whereof may be read in his book what he suffered, and how he slew his foul tyrant and fled to Russia. So, the wars at an end, Anas Todkill is back in Kent, where he tells of his strange adventures, and thinks his peaceful days irksome. The happy hop fields and the maidens are not the fields (or maids) for him; night and morn a voice cries, —

"Awake, thou that sleepest! There be work in the world to do!"

'Till at last there is naught left but to listen to that voice which will not rest. So I say to my old mother:—

"Bless your loving Anas, mother; he must leave you for a season. England calls on all true Englishmen, and would have each do his duty: namely, rifle Spanish galleons or other work in God's cause against the Divell."

*Anas bis
Pilgrimage.*
Thereat my dear old mother wept sore and would not be comforted; but I, that was a man, stood steadfast, though nigh choking.

So this mother and son clasp, and kiss, and part each with other; and Anas Todkill turns his back on the happy autumn fields and goes forth with long thoughts on his Pilgrimage.

II.

*I talk with Captain Smith and Master Shake-
speare at the Mermaid.*

SO I go away to London ; then as now I meet with Captain Smith.
the mighty heart whence the great
pulsations drove the hot blood to the
farthest lands, wherever floated the flag of
England to flout the Spaniard.

When I pass under Temple Bar, I see
Fleet Street full of people ; most of soldiers
from the wars of the Low Countries and
Transylvania. They walk in long strides,
rattling broadswords and twisting mustaches ; each asking other what was coming for them in the new reign of his Majesty King James. I who had been to
London and attended the theatres (though
I be a Puritan) could see many *Nyms* and
Bardolphs in this red-nosed crowd, and
jostled against such. Sudden, a loud voice
greets me, and a hand is struck in mine. I
look up, and who should I see but that
same valiant Captain John Smith, with
bright eyes and long mustaches and beard

His brave apparel.

like a spade, I had last seen in Transylvania when I fell half dead there.

The eyes laughed like the mouth that
said : —

"Anas Todkill! By my faith thou art
welcome, comrade !"

With which he puts one arm round me,
his brave new doublet with rich slashes
and gold lace rubbing up against my country frieze.

" See the gallant !" I say, looking with
lurking smiles at all this bravery ; " the old
soldier turned courtier !"

"And fine gentleman, by my faith !"
he cries, twisting his long mustache. " Why
not ? Duke Sigismund gave me fifteen
hundred gold ducats at Leipzig, Anas.
Hold ! there is your share, comrade."

Whereat he draws from his doublet a
handful of gold which he would thrust on
me, but I would not.

"Well here is your Peru, comrade, when-
ever you will," he says in his gallant voice ;
"and now walk with me, and tell me of
yourself."

So we walked on together and begun
a legion of old stories to renew acquaintance. My own was soon related, and
Smith then tells me how he was made

prisoner and sold to slavery, but killed his He tells of his adventures. tyrant by beating out his brains, when he wandered into the desert, but got to Russia and thence to England. At Leipzig Duke Sigismund gives him the ducats and his patent of Knighthood. He pulls this out now and shows me it in Latin, and says he will have it registered in Garter King of Arms his office.*

"I have deeply hazarded myself, Anas, in doing and suffering," he says, "and even the playwriters make relations of me."

"The playwriters?" I say.

"Yes verily,—is not that the Puritan twang, Anas? They have acted my fatal tragedies on the stage and wracked my relations at their pleasure." †

"Then the rumour has come hither?"

"Doubtless, since they make a play of me. But I owe them no great grudge. Never were better or gentler people than these play actors and writers. Even now I am going to meet one of them, Master Will Shakespeare, who seeks speech with me. Will you go also?"

---

* It was registered there, but not until afterwards, August 19, 1625. The patent signed by Sigismund Bathori at Leipzig in 1603, just before the meeting with Todkill, is given, in the original Latin, in Smith's *True Travels and Adventures*. It is also found in the Harleian MSS., in the British Museum.

† Smith makes the same statement in the same words in the dedication of his *True Travels* to the Earl of Pembroke.

Thereat I laughed and cried : —

"Go see a writer of plays ! I, the godly Anas Todkill ? 'T is sure a snare of Satan. Thou wilt take me to some tavern."

"To the *Mermaid.*"

"The haunt of roysterers, Ben Jonson and his crew! Next, my soul will be imperilled by attending the Globe theatre. Avaunt! Natheless — natheless — I will go."

"I knew thou wouldst ! Catch old birds with chaff, my worthy Puritan ; thou art no better than the rest !"

He laughed loud as before, and putting his arm through mine we go toward the tavern. I was more than willing, for I loved the thought of seeing sweet Will Shakespeare, of whom I had heard much. My Captain now breaks forth in praises of him as we walk along.

"Even you vile Puritan people," he says, "must love him as much as the gayest gallant that ruffles feathers. Sure a greater English pen never wrote than Will Shakespeare's. We will talk with him a little ; then I have somewhat to say to thee, Anas. I want good men for a great work ; but more anon of that."

We come at last to the *Mermaid* tavern

and find the place full of swordsmen rattling spurs and drinking sack, and talking loud of their exploits in the Flanders wars. My Captain pushes through 'em as one who is weary of that, and goes to a corner where is seated in a sort of shadow a man with a bald forehead and a pointed beard, in a turned down collar. He is looking at the crowd and smiling in a notable way, and as I gaze at him I think, "He is studying these people." This man, I soon found, was Master Will Shakespeare; and not far from him sate a burly big man with a pocked face drinking sack, who was the great playwriter, Ben Jonson. *Sweet Will Shakespeare and Rare Ben Jonson.*

As we now begin talking with Master Shakespeare, Master Jonson chimes in, and they two have wit combats; wherein Shakespeare is like a quiet English craft darting to and fro around a huge Spanish galleon, firing culverins into her hulk. When Smith first comes up Master Shakespeare rises and salutes him, smiling. His smile is extraordinary sweet, and his way of speaking very simple and friendly. They talked a long time, but Master Shakespeare listened more than he spoke. With his eyes fixed on Smith he seemed to be studying him too, as he had been studying the crowd in the tavern, where that day came *Ancient Pistol*, and one resembling Sir *John Falstaff*, though methinks that wonder of wit must have been a pure fancy of the brain.

. The talk went on to the afternoon, and I well remember all Master Shakespeare said. He was ever smiling and sipping his sack, and when Master Ben Jonson cried "Ho! ho!" and jested in his deep, gruff voice at his friend, Master Shakespeare turns round sudden and fires a shot at him. But for having much to record, I should beg the good reader to so far bear with me as to let me set down the exact words of Master Shakespeare, the jests he uttered, and some wondrous maxims that came from him. But time is wanting, and I needs must pass to that audience with which I was honoured on this same day by his Majesty King James. It were ill to spend attention on a mere play-writer while his gracious Majesty waits. So I pass over what Master Shakespeare told us of his life at Stratford, why he came up to London, and where he got his plays. He spoke of all to Smith, who was not a stranger to him; and had I space I might tell the names of the real people he drew from, in tragedy and comedy, from *Shy-* *lock*, the Jew of Venice, to wheezy Sir *John Falstaff*, who so exceeds all else for wit and humour that I have seen the great crowds at the Globe, or the House in Black Friars, rise up and shout as he waddled on the stage.

To end with Master Shakespeare whose fine filed talk I could set down. His discourse with Smith was of a drama which he purposed writing on his return to Stratford, which always inspired him, he said, as one to the mannor born.* This drama, meant to be writ, he said, would be named "The Tempest," and the stage to be the Bermudas, or *Isles of Devils*, whereof Master Henry May, the shipwrecked mariner, writes in his relation of 1593, then late printed.† Somewhat more was needed, Master Shakespeare said, than that brief relation ; and he prayed Captain Smith, if he ever visited this wild country, to come to Stratford on Avon when he was back in England, and tell him all things at his New Place house there. This and more was

---

* The spelling of the word "manor" in this place by Todkill would seem to indicate that Shakespeare wrote "to the *mannor* born," and not "to the *manner*," in Hamlet. The word manor is so spelled in old deeds of that century and the century succeeding it.

† In 1600, just preceding this interview with Shakespeare.

We take leave of that wonder.

said : how the Captain should be a welcome guest there, and how himself, Master Shakespeare, spent his time: in what hours of the day he writes his plays, and how they would come to him ; brief, all about himself, and how his life passed there. But for having greater matter, — that audience with his Majesty, — I might here trifle the time for my reader (though he were loth) with this small, idle gossip touching a writer of plays. Sure that were a shame, Anas (I say), while his Majesty waits! Think! thy dread liege, King James, to wait on a player !

So at last this sweet Will Shakespeare takes leave of us with close pressure of hands ; goes away to the town of Stratford, where he seemeth to think naught of his fame ; and now, lately, falls asleep there, and lies under the daisies. Almost I doubt it had not been better to forget his great Majesty and speak of this Shakespeare ; of his flashes of quick conceit and weighty thoughts winged with laughter. Natheless, Smith would go to the King, and we push through the Nyms and Pistols out of the *Mermaid:* but he, too, pondereth and saith, turning to look back : " Is he not wonderful, this sweet Will Shakespeare ? Was there ever a kindlier smile? No marvel *Smith would visit the Virgin Land.* his plays ravish the listeners with a sort of delight."

"Well, perchance he hath some merit," I say, designing a jest; "he is the best of his bad class, I allow."

Thereat Smith burst forth in laughter.

" There is godly Anas Todkill making believe he is a hater of plays and play-writers, and loves 'em all the time, though he scoff at 'em! But to other matters, Anas. I am going on the Virginia voyage."

"The Virginia voyage!" I say.

" Yea, though it end at the Isle of Devils, — the *still-vex'd Bermoothes*, as Master Shakespeare called them."

" "Avaunt Sathanas!" I cry; "thou wilt lead me to perdition."

" No, to the Virgin land, Anas! Come, I want men like thee. Worthy Bartholomew Gosnold, the brave sea captain, and my friend, hath set on foot a voyage thither to found a colony in the wondrous country. . Fame surely hath told you of him. He it was who made the first straight voyage across the Atlantic ocean. He landed in New England, but would now adventure farther south. This voyage fills my mind,

I have audience of his gracious majesty.

comrade. That country is now untrod, but who knows? great cities and states may some day rise there. It may be, the world rolls westward, not eastward as some will have it. Master Gosnold has got three ships — the *God Speed*, the *Susan Constant*, and the *Discovery* — and a hundred adventurers. Wilt thou go with him and me? If thou wilt, Anas, we shall see fine times! All is ready. Even now I seek his Majesty, who has granted us his patent. Come thou, too, and talk with him; fear not! 't is only a man, and not so much a man, for *thy* ear, Anas!"

Whoso listened to this soldier was sooner or later persuaded by him. I was ready for that same persuasion. There was nought to hold me in England, and I longed to sail the western seas and reach the wondrous land, and find the Fount of Youth there, wherein I believed, nor am sure I disbelieve to-day. So I joyfully agreed to go on this famous Virginia voyage; and went with Captain Smith to Whitehall, where we had audience of his Majesty about the Virginia business. I, Anas Todkill, was ushered in with him, and his Majesty speaks to me by name in his sweet Scottish accent. But this great

and exceeding honour deserveth more rela- *A full re-*
tion : and now see how ill a thing it had *pertory thereof.*
been to waste time on Master Shakespeare !
There had then been no space to tell of
this far greater honour, — my audience
with his Majesty, whereof I give here a
full repertory of all he said, leaving out
nothing.* . . .

* Unfortunately the sheets of Master Todkill's relation describ-
ing his interview with King James I. have been lost. The paging
indicates that the relation was elaborate.

III.

I go on the Virginia Voyage, and what followed at Jamestown.

SO at last the adventurers to Virginia were on the ocean; and passing the Azores, sailed westward to the unknown land. The spring was come as we neared Mevis, Mona, and the Virgin Isles, and the sea was ruffled to silver ripples by the south wind. Here we rested, and then went on, coasting the country of Florida (where the Spaniard hath intruded), smelling the perfume of early flowers wafted far out to sea. The colony was to be fixed at Roanoke, where that valiant and great spirit, Sir Richard Grenville of noble memory — he who fought the fifty Spaniards in his one ship, the *Revenge*, off the Azores, and died with a quiet mind * — founded

* This is evidently an allusion to the last words of Sir Richard Grenville, whose famous combat with the Spanish ships had taken place about fifteen years before : —

" Here I, Richard Grenville, die with a joyous and quiet mind, for that I have ended my life as a true soldier ought to do, fighting for his country, queen, religion, and honour, my soul willingly departing from this body, leaving behind the lasting fame of having behaved as every valiant soldier is in his duty bound to do."

the first English colony. The poor people wandered off into the woods and were nevermore heard of, — a strange decree of Almighty Providence, were aught done by Him strange, or not a working together for good to them that love Him. So they went away quietly, — little Virginia Dare, the first English child born in America, and the rest, — and the cypress forest took them, and they were no more heard of.

And enter the sea of Chesapeake, called of the Spaniard Santa Maria.

Now this old Roanoke colony was to be built again on the same foundation. But we were never to see Roanoke. A fierce storm drave us northward to the mouth of a great bay, and taking refuge therein we thanked God for his deliverance, and resolved to found the Virginia colony here.

Before us was a great inland sea, with waves as high as the main ocean, over which skimmed white-winged sea-fowl, and along the shore was a fringe of goodly trees. Sailing on, we named a cape of land Point Comfort, since we had good comfort there after the tossing storm ; and then we went up a great river, called the Powhatan by the Indians, and landed here and there in the Paspahegh country, the land of Appomattocks, and elsewhere, looking for a good spot. This we found on the

2

left bank of the river about forty miles from its mouth, and here we landed in May, calling the place Jamestown in honour of his Majesty, and pitched tents, and set to work building cabins.

If the readers of this true relation would know of the old times at Jamestown, — how we lived under tents and boughs, and stretched a canvas between trees to worship God under, with a pulpit of a bar of wood nailed to two of the trunks ; and worked at the huts with dusky Indians looking on, and wondering at the reed thatching as at us and all we did, — this is writ in the old repertories of Master Fenton, Master George Percy, and other of Smith's old soldiers.

This true relation tells the story of my Lady Pokahontas ; but natheless comes back to memory that fearful summer of our blessed Lord, 1607. A hot fever, bred of the river ooze and sultry sun, well nigh destroyed us. For five months in this miserable distress there were not five men to man the bulwarks ; in every corner of the fort old soldiers groaning day and night most pitiful to hear. If there be any conscience in men it would make their hearts to bleed, could I tell them of the pitiful murmuring of our poor sick men, by *The terrible* *fever.* day and by night ; some departing out of the world, many times three and four in a night ! in the morning the dead bod- ies trailed out of the cabins like dogs, to be buried in the ooze by the rest of the sick, scarce enough to perform that sad office.*

Oh, it was pitiful, and but for our Cap- tain, Smith, the end of the colony had then come. He it was who, next under God, preserved us all from death and confusion. When not ten men could go or stand, he fed the sick and was the head of all. Of that fearful time I can speak no further. My breast still labours to think how, ere the autumn of that year, we lost one half our company. But the cool days came at last, and the rivers were full of wild fowls, giving meat to our starving handful.

Hope revived with this blessed season, and next, the Council bethink them that his Majesty's command to discover the South Sea beyond the Blue Mountains is not obeyed yet.

Now a word of this same Council, — not much speaking, since they be not worthy of

* This account exactly agrees with that of George Percy, brother of the Earl of Northumberland, in his *Discourse of the Plantation of the Southern Colony in Virginia.*

Smith seeketh the great South Sea. it. The head thereof was Master Edward Maria Wingfield, a fat merchant, and the tail, one Ratcliffe, a counterfeit impostor, as will be set forth. This Wingfield had been best at home, for his heart failed him from the first, and he did nought but feast on the stores, and start at shadows, thinking Smith would murder him. Smith haunts him night and day; would make himself " King of Virginia," and is tried on that charge, and Wingfield shown to have suborned perjury. So the jury acquits Smith and puts Ratcliffe in Wingfield's stead; when he would seize the Pinnace and fly to England, whither the two other ships had gone, as I will relate.

Now these Councillors would destroy their enemy, the valiant Captain Smith, and urged the South Sea discovery in the bitter season to that end. But he, full of his brave spirit, natheless would undertake it; or at least go and explore the river Chickahomania, which hath its head in the Blue Mountains, beyond which is the great South Sea, though none hath discovered it. So toward the time of Christmas, in the middle of an extreme frost, Smith sets out in his barge, like old Ulysses, with companions, and sails westward toward the baths of the stars, and is no more seen for *The bruit comes be is slain.* a long season.

Fain would I, Anas Todkill, have made one of his mariners, for my heart cleaved to this valiant soldier ; but I could not, being sick of a quinsy, and was forced to tarry at Jamestown. Soon the white sail of the barge was seen coming back down the James River ; and the men, all bleeding and distraught, bring a report that Smith is slain by the savages and two others with him. Thereat a great grief smote me, and I cried :—

"Farewell thou good soldier ! None hath seen thy like, and will not in the time to come ! "

Master Wingfield is standing by, puffing out with his pursy mouth, as I say this, and scowls at me. The new President, Ratcliffe, hears me too, and looks at me with his bloodshot eyes under bushy black brows.

" Cease thy muttering ! " growls this Ratcliffe ; " Smith is a traitor, whose end is just."

" He is no traitor ! " I cry, " but a true man and a worthy. It is they who devour the stores and spend the days in riotous living, while we starve, who are the traitors ! "

Thereat some standing by frown and mutter: —

"Anas Todkill says the truth!"

When Ratcliffe falls in a rage and shouts :

"Arrest this brawler and mutineer!"

"Arrest him, I say!" here cries Wingfield, red with wrath, to his confederate, Archer; and claps me in the Fort, where I lay till past New Year in arrest.*

By that time all was combustion and confusion at Jamestown. The unruly crew ruled all and ruined all. Then the last black act comes. Wingfield, Ratcliffe, and Archer seize the Pinnace to escape to England.

But their evil hour had come. It was now past New Year, and the ground was white with snow, when sudden the bruit runs, "Smith is coming!" Thereat I, who was yet under arrest, pushed by the man on guard at the Fort, dared him to stop me, caring nought, and rushed out and met Smith, who strides into the palisade with a wild train of heathen.†

Short work is made of the confederates, who had hastened on board the Pinnace

---

* Wingfield had no right to arrest Todkill, having been deposed; but his confederate, Archer, chose, it seems, to regard the order as sufficient, all the more as Ratcliffe had also given it.

† These heathen or Indians were the friendly guides and attendants supplied to Smith by Powhatan.

and would have fled. But Smith runs to the Fort and trains cannon on the ship ; nor stops he to summon them. His friends crowd around him, and sudden the culverins roar. With sakre-falcon and musket-shot he thunders on those mutineers, and they have notice to stay or sink. They surrender and come on shore, a black looking crew enough ; but many are their followers, so that Smith is not master yet. He is like to be victim even. The very next day he is *arraigned for trial under the law of Leviticus* for the death of the two men slain on the Chickahomania! I who write this, long after, stop and shake with laughter at that. But it was done : his enemies would try him, alleging the Levitical law that he should be put to death! *

Smith is tried by the Levitical Law.

But their horns were so much too short to finish that business. Smith was not the man to trifle the time with such tuftaffty humourists. Sudden the whole party, judges and all, are arrested. Then Smith, sword in hand, points to the river and says : —

" To the Pinnace ! Since these gallants

---

* This statement of Todkill's is fully corroborated in the *General History*, where it is said : " Some no better than they should be plotted the next day to have put him to death by the Levitical law," for having " led to their ends " the two victims.

But that ends badly. like it so, they shall live there at my pleasure, till I send them home to be tried by
the High Council."

Thereat the old soldiers shout and
clash swords round the chief,
and the confederates are
forced on the Pinnace,
and Smith is
master.

IV.

My Captain tells how an Angel saved Him.

SO this ill business is over, and all re- Smith's peril with the heathen.
joice that Smith is back. The gallant
face is a stay to the feeble, and new life-
blood seemeth to flow in the veins of the
poor people. He ordereth all things for
peace or war; and, that done, comes to the
Fort in the sunset, where I am on post.
When the guard relieves me we walk on
the shore.

"I will tell thee of a great hazard I have
run, Anas," Smith says. And then, with a
wistful look, he acquaints me how he was
seized by the heathen in the Chickahomania desert, and tied to a tree to be
shot with arrows, but he showed them an
ivory dial. Seeing the needle through the
glass and yet unable to touch it, they think
him a god. So they spared him and conducted him to their great Emperor, the
mighty King Powhatan, at his royal resi-
dence on the York River.

"Never was such a sight, Anas," the gal-

*He is led be-
fore their
Emperor.*
lant Captain says. " The Emperor, with no beard and a sour look, was sitting in his great arbour or wigwam, with his guard of one hundred bowmen, who surround him day and night. At his head and foot were beautiful Indian girls, his favourite wives, with other women ranged in long rows against the wall, with naked shoulders dyed with puccoon, and white bracelets. The Emperor himself was clad in a robe of raccoon skin, and spoke some words in their strange language. Soon I found what was meant to be done with me, Anas. They brought in a huge stone and dragged me to it, and forced me down on it. Then a big savage raised his club to beat out my brains, when God's mercy sent to my suc-cour one of his angels."

Thereat I, who had listened intently, gave a great start and exclaimed : —

"Sent one of his angels ! Natheless 't is not impossible, since we read of such things in the Holy Book. Tell me further."

" The angel was a girl of twelve or thir-teen, the King's beloved daughter. I had taken note of her in the throng for her extreme grace and comeliness, far exceed-ing for beauty the rest of her people.*

* Smith makes a similar statement in his published description of Pokahontas.

She was clad in a doeskin robe lined with down from the breast of the wood-pigeon, with bracelets of coral, and a white plume in her black hair. She was short and slight of stature with feet so small as scarce carried her; and I protest to you, Anas, I have seen many English maidens worse favoured and proportioned than my little angel." *

"You do well to call her such. She saved you then, this child?" I say, wondering.

"She ran and clasped my head and held me close to her heart that was beating, and looks up to her father the Emperor, begging he will spare me."

"A great wonder, but God is merciful."

"Certes He it was who sent her. For with tears streaming down she holds me close to her bosom, and murmurs pitifully that I be spared."

"And he listens to her?"

"He leans on his hand, and muses a little space. Then he holds out his big red arm, and he with the club falls back, sudden. I am saved, Anas!"

Much wondering at this strange relation, I say:—

* See Smith's letter to the Queen

" What might be this angel's name ? "

" She hath three, whereof Pokahontas and Amonate be two. The third, which is her real name, none would tell me, lest I cast spells on her." *

" The heathen savages that toy with fancies ! "

" Toy say you? Well the great King Powhatan would have me stay and fashion toys for the maiden. A strange business for him that was an old soldier of Duke Sigismund, but not irksome, Anas ! So I that was to be clubbed to death was now safe, and feasted royally, and all my business was to fashion trinkets with my jack-knife for my little beauty ! Do you laugh at me, Anas ? She is a beauty, and though she made signs to me that she was thirteen only, I should have thought her a maid of seventeen. These dusky flowers bloom early, far earlier than our English lasses. And you should have seen Pokahontas bending over me with her brown face all aglow as I worked, and her slim arms with the coral bracelets reaching out from a robe of feathers of forest birds to take the trinket I fashioned ! Sure never was young fawn of the fallow deer more graceful than this tender virgin ! "

* This was a superstition of the Virginia Indians.

Thereat I laugh, for as he speaks thus *I warn my Captain to beware.* Smith's face glows, and I suspect something.

"A dusky wonder!" I say. "So you love her even now?"

"Love her, say you, Anas!" he replies, looking at me curiously; "sure I love her since she saved me."

But I, shaking my head:—

"That is not the love a man loves a woman with; and this maid is a woman sith you call her seventeen in face and looks. Beware, worthy Captain!"

Smith laughed and blushed a little, and said:—

"That were too foolish, Anas!"

"Remember you are young," I say.

"I am twenty-nine this very month, of this very year."

"An age to kindle!"

"By my faith thou hast lost thy head, Anas!" he says. "What time have I to love, or think to marry any woman? For look you, Anas, poor soldier as I am, I would live *par amours* with none of them."

"Certes I believe that, knowing you as I do," I say; "and to marry this dusk princess were a deadly sin, good Captain."

" A sin, Anas ? "

He turns his head and looks at me of a sudden.

" Surely a sin, since the Holy Book forbids marriage with strange wives, and this Pokahontas belongs to a cursed generation."

At this he muses a little, holding his chin in his hand, and that elbow in the tother * hand.

" Well, set thy mind at ease," he says at last ; " I shall see her no more."

" Who knoweth ? "

" She is but a child and would not venture through the irksome woods."

Thereat I laugh and say : —

" But thou — thou wilt venture to *her*, I think ! "

He blushes and looking sideways says to me : —

" Cease, thou foolish Anas ! nevermore shall I see this blessed Pokahontas in any coming time."

But sudden a bruit sounds from the forest near and Smith turns and looks.

" She is come ! " he cries out, his face

* This pleonasm is common in the old writings to the time of Bacon's rebellion. In urging his famous Middle Plantation oath, he asks his auditors how many of them Sir William Berkley is apt to dispatch, for what they have already done, to " the tother world."

glowing. "She is yonder, in the woods! *With bas-kets.*
See her slim figure, Anas, and the white
plume in her black hair ! "

"And a wild train with baskets of somewhat to eat," I laugh, — " the angel ! "

V.

How I first see my Lady Pokahontas.

My Captain's fawn of the woods.

THE angel comes out of the woods with her wild train of attendants, and the full baskets weigh down the backs of the dusky people. They were full-grown and brawny, with coverings of deer and bear skin, but I was looking at the osier baskets of corn and venison.

The maid comes toward us, stepping with a pretty and proud gait, like a fawn. Her hair was black and straight, but scarce seen for the broad white plume in it. Now I knew that my Captain had spoken truth of her face and form, for scarce have I in England seen maid so beautiful. She comes putting down each little foot, covered with bead moccasins, light but firm, and smiling out of black eyes.

Smith's tanned face glowed as his eyes met hers, and he went forward with out-stretched hands. Thereat she blushes also, and gives him her hands, looking at him and studying his face, but speaking

no word. Smith bows down his head, kissing the hand of the small princess, and
then he leads her into the Fort, and they
discourse together by signs. It was a marvel to see how quickly she understood and
made her own meaning plain. She gazed
about in wonder, more than all at the cannon ; and when Smith, for her better entertainment, orders a culverin to be dis-
charged into the trees covered with icicles,
she starts, putting her hands to her ears,
and sudden draws close to him as though
for protection.

She came in the morning early, and went
back to her heathen abode on the great
river a little past noon. To the Emperor's
city was but a short fourteen miles, and she
passed through the wondering crowd and
went her way. She and Smith parted with
hands joined together, and looking each in
other's eyes. Was my fancy true ? I could
not tell at that time. Had a Christian man
fallen in love with a heathen girl ? The
Lord forbid that ! I said. But I could see
that the maid had lost her heart to the
young soldier.

Now this sudden passion, or else her
own kind heart, was God's blessing to us
poor people, in dire distress for food ; for

3

the stores were now all spent, and but for
the corn and venison brought in the baskets, many had surely perished of mere
famine.   It was true what Smith writ afterwards in his letter to her Majesty the Queen
that, without this tender virgin and her
great heart to succour us, this fine land of
Virginia had lain as at our first arrival till
this day; for she, next under God, was still
the instrument to preserve the colony from
death, famine, and utter confusion.* Every
few days thereafter she comes back with
her osier baskets filled, and the starving
men blessed this love of dear Pokahontas.

More of this perilous time I need not
here set down.   Often thinking of it, I
shudder in my limbs, and thank God for
Pokahontas.   "But for her," I say again
and again as I ponder, " this goodly heri-
tage of Virginia had sunk back in heathen-
dom, and God's immortal cause have had
herein no exemplar."

Happily succour soon arrives.   A white
sail comes up the great river, flying the
English flag ; and seeing she was not a
Spaniard, but from the home land, a roar of
culverins salutes her, and she comes to anchor.   Her commander was Captain New-

* Smith uses the same words in his letter to the Queen.

port, an empty, idle man, who was ever *Newport's ship.*
carrying tales to the Company in London ;
but we cared not, since they sent us new
men and supplies for our poor colony.

VI.

The Strange Antics of Pokahontas.

Her gambols at James-town. IN the years to come, when this fair land of America, as the new fashion is to call Virginia, shall be full of men and women, and great cities rise in the wilds, — which doubtless will come to pass in the long hours of the future, — these first struggles of the Virginia colony for mere existence will touch all hearts. I, who write this, cannot draw the moving picture of that time, since 't is only to tell of my lady Pokahontas that I write this relation.

She was ever in and out of the James-town palisade with her wild train, gambolling mirthfully on the grass, and looking at all things around her with curious eyes. What I marvelled at most was the child and the woman mixed in her. Sure never was such a mingling; but Smith had said truly. It was more a maiden of seventeen than a child that I saw in these days; and never in any of her plays and antics was there any freedom or immodesty. She was

decently clad in her robe of birds' feathers, *The gilded dirt.*
and wore a girdle from the waist below the
knees. On her feet were beaded moccasins, as these people call their shoes, and
never saw I the maid's shoulders, which she
kept wrapped to the chin in her soft robe.
Above showed a dusk face with a small
mouth, and a nose very slight and straight.
Her eyes were black, and had an extreme
softness; her hair of the same colour and
with never a curl in it, in which drooped
down a plume of white feathers, her badge
of princess.

She soon caught a few words of English, and then learned wondrous fast. She
spoke with a curious lisp or murmuring of
the lips, but not ungainly. She and Smith
much affected each other, and always the
same glow was on her face as she looked
at him; but in his I could read nothing.
A mild sweetness and kindness was all writ
there, however I sought to find more.

It was not a time for dalliance when men
were muttering and falling into mutiny,
and the strong hand was all that kept the
factions from springing and grappling each
with other. Newport's ships were now to
return, and a craze seized on the company
that had found in the neighbourhood of

Jamestown a yellow dirt they thought to be gold. Pokahontas told us 't was nought, but Newport and the rest lost their heads. There was no talk or hope but to dig gold, wash gold, refine gold, and load gold. Smith went about telling them hotly he was not enamoured of their dirty skill, and murmuring at their neglect of all business to fraught the drunken ship with their gilded dirt. These words and others he said, breathing out his passion ; but Newport would not listen, and sailed away with a cargo of the fantastical dirt, which, once at London, was found worthless (as Pokahontas said), and mere dirt indeed.

This and other old recollections come back as I now write, — with the voyages on the Chesapeake, where Smith with fourteen men in his open barge sailed three thousand miles. We stopped to visit on the Eastern Shore the laughing King of Accomac, who told us of two dead children there, on whose faces whoso looked presently fell down and died. Then we sailed to the head of the bay, and back up Patawamak ; thence to Rappahannock, where the savages came to fight us, carrying boughs of trees to cover them, and I was shot with an arrow, and all bloody, and nigh having my brains beat out. So back *We make him our President.* around Point Comfort, where a dread tempest struck us, and we could only see the shore in the dark night by the lightning flashes; but God preserved us, in his great mercy, and we came back to Jamestown, where all were starving, and the new President, Ratcliffe, was feasting on the stores, and building himself a palace for pleasure in the woods near.*

This so moved our dead spirits that we presently deposed him, and made Smith President, who set all to work, stopping the pleasure house, and warning Master Ratcliffe at his peril to hold his peace and labour with the rest.

Then came Newport back from England, and would crown the Emperor Powhatan under-King, subject to his Majesty, which was done. Never was sight so curious. But to speak first of our strange meeting again with Pokahontas.

Captain Newport, a vain, idle man, fearful of his shadow (he blackened us to the people in London, for which we loved him little), sent Smith with a party to Werowocomoco to summon the Emperor to James-

* Todkill was one of the authors of the detailed relations of the Chesapeake voyages in the *General History of Virginia, New England, and the Summer Isles*, 1624.

town to be crowned.   Arriving at York River, which we crossed in Indian boats, we found the Emperor away, and sent word we had come, and so waited.   We were in a broad field nigh some woods, seated by a fire, when sudden came a bruit from the woods, a hideous noise and shrieking, that we ran to arms, looking for an attack.   But no one designed attacking us.   Instead came Pokahontas flitting like a fawn out of the woods, and running to Smith seized his hands and laughed, with her head bent sidewise.

"They shall not hurt," she lisped in her poor English.   "If they hurt, he shall kill Matoaka." *

As she said "he," she touched Smith lightly on the breast and then touched her own bosom.   She was truly a wondrous sight.   She had small deer antlers on her head, and a robe of otter skin around her shoulders; another fell from her waist near to her beaded moccasins on her small feet. At her back was a quiver of arrows, and she had a small cedar bow in her hand. Flourishing this around her head, she flitted back, still laughing, to the woods, and

---

* This was the *real name* of Pokahontas, which her family had not divulged to Smith.

soon appeared a party of girls, nigh a score, *Her merry* *masquerade.* singing and dancing, their bodies painted with many colours, with girdles of green leaves from the waist down, all horned like Pokahontas, and flourishing swords and potsticks. Never was such a sight! I near died for laughing. The fair fiends rushed out with most hellish shouts and cries, and danced in ring about the fire, their hands joined together, and all laughing. Then after an hour spent in this masquerade, they danced away and were lost to sight, Pokahontas going last, and looking over her shoulder.

Smith claps his hands and says to me : —

"Well, what think you of this, Anas? Lift up your testimony against these heathen, my worthy Puritan!"

"The heathen are not ill favoured," I say, "but sing in excellent ill variety."

"A truce to growls, Anas!" Smith says laughing; "here they come as before."

With that appeared Pokahontas at the head of her maidens, but divested of their strange devices, with intent to invite us to supper, which was spread in a neighbouring arbour. Here the Indian girls flocked around, handing venison in wooden plat-

ters, crowding and crying most tediously
" Love you not me ? " to Smith and all.
Whereat Pokahontas was much displeased
and rated them soundly for their ill man-
ners; which I could see from her flushed
face and royal air as of a princess, though
I understood not her barbarous language.
After supper we were conducted to our
lodgings, — Indian girls carrying torches
before us, and then going back, — and so
rested in sound sleep after this laughing
masquerade.*

The Emperor comes next day and re-
ceives Smith, holding out both hands, with
many pretty discourses, to renew old acquaintance. He sat on his bed of mats with
a handsome young woman at his head and
feet, and around him were his warriors and
wives, their heads and shoulders painted
red. I much marvelled at this savage state
and his kingly words when Smith invited
him to Jamestown to be crowned. He
would not go thither.

" If your King hath sent me presents,"
he said by his interpreter, "I also am a
King and this is my land. Eight days I
will stay to receive them. Your Father

---

¹ Todkill is the author also of the description of this scene, in the
General History.

Newport is to come to me, not I to him, *Is crowned under-King Powhatan I.* nor yet to your Fort; neither bite I at such a bait."

To this he held and would not come; so we went back, and Newport returned to Powhatan with us, and the savage was crowned King. I, Anas Todkill, Puritan, and not so much a king lover, laughed mightily. Sure never was stranger sight. The old heathen accepted the bason and bedding sent him and was pleased, I could see, to have them. But when Captain Newport essayed to put a scarlet cloak on him he grunted and resisted. Much worse was it when they signed to him to bend his knee that he might be crowned. He would not. He rose straighter and looked scornful, but at last his werowances leaned on his shoulders and he was forced to kneel and be crowned. As they put it on his head a sign was made and a volley was fired; whereat the new king started up and would have caught up his royal hatchet, thinking it an attack.

Then I, who had stood by laughing, began to laugh more than ever. The old Emperor went up to Newport and congratulated his kindness, then looking very solemn he gives Newport his old shoes and

We go back. raccoon skin robe as a present to King James, in return for his crown !

Ere we went back to Jamestown I saw no further of Pokahontas, and was not to see her again till past New Year, when she showed me her brave heart and made me what I am, and will be, until death takes me, her faithful liegeman.

VII.

Of God's Mercy to his Unworthy Servant through the Blessed Pokahontas.

IT comes about in this wise. Now Newport, after that vain march to the Moncan country, goes back to England, taking with him Ratcliffe and Wingfield ; and he snow was falling, and the colony had o corn. We must have that, or the men tarve, and needs must when the Divell lrives. *We go in search of corn.*

No persuasion can persuade Smith to tarve, and he goes down to Nansemunge, nd says, " Give me corn ; " but the heathen vill not. They have orders (they say) from King Powhatan to refuse us ; and seeing lainly what this means, Captain Smith vill go and see the King, with fifty good hot.

Powhatan himself gives reason for coming. He sends inviting Captain Smith, nd praying he will send men to build him house, and certain Dutch men go by the and way, and Smith by water. So with

Are warned on the way of Powhatan's intent. Master George Percy, brother of his lordship the Earl of Northumberland, and other brave gentlemen and fighters to the number of fifty, Smith sails in the Pinnace round Point Comfort into the great York River, saying to me, as we pass, " Here is a spot for a York Town which may perchance one day be built and grow to be famous."

But ever as we sail, stopping here and there to see the Indian people, comes a warning what Powhatan would do. The King of Worrosqueake says to our Captain : —

" Captain Smith, you shall find Powhatan to use you kindly, but trust him not."

" I will not," says our Captain in his soldier way.

" And be sure," says the King, " he have no opportunity to seize your arms, for he hath sent for you only to cut your throats."

The Captain thanks him for his good counsel, but says he will see to that ; and so we leave them. Certes, Smith was glad to know of the Emperor's intent. It seemed ill going to put his hand on one who invited him to Werowocomoco (the heathen capital). But sith the host would cut the throat of the guest, there was no such harm

in doing the same (perchance) to him, likewise.

So the Pinnace goes on, a little past the time of Christmas, and sails up York River, with the barge following, to Werowocomoco, which in their tongue signifieth the "Chief Place of Council."

Powhatan meets Smith in his great wigwam, but not with pretty discourse to renew old acquaintance as before. Why had we come? he says in a muttered voice, with cold looks. He had no corn. His people had none. But for forty swords he would supply three hundred bushels.

Smith standing in the midst shakes his head; swords were a bad traffic with so subtle an enemy. So they argue to and fro but come to no conclusion, till in the end Powhatan promises the corn if the Englishmen will come ashore for it *without their arms, which frighted his poor people.* Then his meaning was plain; and Smith, seeing the Emperor did but trifle the time to cut his throat, goes to the door of the wigwam and fires off his pistol, which was the signal to come on shore and surprise Powhatan.

Sudden the barge was heard breaking the ice on the way from the Pinnace, for the river was frozen near half a mile from

either shore. Thereat Powhatan took fright
and was quickly gone out of his wigwam ;
and the savages made an attack, which but
for Smith had surely ended us. He cut
out his way, sword in hand, and we following him gained the shore, where we in-
trenched till morning.

Now followed a new proof of the love of
that blessed Pokahontas. The night was
extreme cold, and we sought a ruined wigwam near, to watch in till daylight. But
Powhatan meant to destroy us, and would
have done so but that the Eternal All-see-
ing God did prevent him.

Sudden in the dark night, through the
irksome woods, came his dearest jewel
and daughter, Pokahontas. She told us
with streaming tears that her father would
send us supper, and while we were eat-
ing fall on and slay us. This she said in
her broken words, with a trembling voice,
holding Smith's hand, as though loth to
let it go lest some mishap befall him.

I well remember his face flushed, and
taking a trinket from his breast he would
give it her ; but she, putting it by, said
with tears that her father would kill her if
he saw her wear it ; and so, covering her
wet eyes, ran away by herself as she came.

The warning was not too soon. Ere long came lusty fellows with platters of bread and venison, but making wry faces at the smoke of our lighted matchlocks, which made them sick (they said). Smith smiled thereat, with a wistful look, thinking doubtless of Pokahontas and what she told him ; and first making the lusty savages eat of the victuals lest they be poisoned, he sent them back to Powhatan with the message he need give himself no more trouble : his plot was discovered.

So no more that night wherein Smith talked apart with me as I watched.

" Is she not a true angel now, Anas ? What think you ? " he says; " know you a court lady who had thus stolen through the dark night to save her friend, — nay the enemy of her people ? I who am only a poor soldier protest to you on my honour, friend, that sith God thus watches over us I think this enterprise be fated to turn out to his glory and the good of his people."

" Doubtless 't is so fated, worthy Captain," I reply, " if they do not slay us on the morrow."

" They will not do that," he says ; " but more force would be better. What say you to find your way to Jamestown for another score of men? It is three hours to daylight, and you may come back past noon."

I rose up at the word and was rowed over in the barge, and then set out walking quickly and reached Jamestown a little past daylight. Ill news awaited me. The day before, Master Scrivener, the new Councillor, had been overturned in a boat and drowned with nine others in James River.

Natheless the men returned with me, and we got back to York River a little past noon, but no Pinnace there, nor Smith. Where had they gone? With much doubt lest they destroy me, I take a canoe I find and cross to a clump of bushes, thinking to meet some friendly Indian who would tell me; when sudden a company rushes out and seizes me, and carries me to Powhatan, who was sitting as before in his great wigwam.

His face was dark, and from the first I saw I was to be slain. Smith had got his corn and gone away to Pamunkey, and the Emperor was raging at what had befell him.

Soon I found that my end was to be the same as that meant for Smith; a stone was brought in, but a sign from the Emperor stopped them. Pokahontas was leaning on his knees talking low to him, and he was listening. Soon he said some words to his people, and I was taken away to a far wigwam, where a guard was put over me.

The black night now comes, and I give myself over for lost, — doubtless they will brain me as I sleep. Sudden steals in, through the guards, who did not stop her, the blessed Pokahontas ; who told me in her broken English that I was to be put to death the next day ; she had begged her father to spare me till then, that I might pray to my Gods ; but now she would save me.

Thereat wondering, I obeyed her sign, and followed her out of the wigwam. The guards were her two brothers, one of them, Nantaquaus, the comeliest savage I ever beheld, and kind, like his sister. These two had plotted my rescue, and went a little way with me in the woods, meaning to whoop when I was safe away, feigning that I had escaped out of the wigwam.

Pokahontas told me where to find Smith, — who had indeed left word for me, — and went full two miles with me and Nantaquaus. Then she took my two hands, and bending close to me, —

We sail back to James-town.

" Fare you well," she says. "When you
see him who calls me ' Child,' tell him why
will he come and make war on my father,
who loves him much, but must destroy
him."

At this tears came into her eyes, and
she went off with Nantaquaus in the dark.
When I had gone some miles further, I
heard a halloo toward Werowocomoco, and
knew how Nantaquaus was giving news of
my escape.   I hurried on, and a little past
midday came to where the York River divideth itself into two gallant branches.
Travelling on I at last found Smith, at a
time when he had seized the Chief Opechancanough by his scalplock in the midst
of his braves.   He ransomed himself with
corn, and so embarking we sailed down
again, and found the men who had come
with me ; and having now sufficient corn,
returned to Jamestown.*

Is it so much to wonder at that thence-
forth I loved the maid who had saved me
in my dire extremity ?   Sure the man
would be ingrate whose heart melted not
at such goodness.   And so I, who had
laughed at Smith for calling the blessed

* Todkill is one of the writers of the relation of these events, also,
in the *General History* ; but arrived too late, it seems, to witness one
of the most remarkable of Smith's exploits.

maiden his guardian angel, now bowed *My saint.*
down before her, and though no vain and
foolish Papist, but a good Puritan of Puritans, made her my Saint Pokahontas.

VIII.

How my Captain loveth the Child of a Cursed Generation.

Peace at last with the Heathen.

ALL this spring of the year 1609, dear Pokahontas, as the old soldiers would still call her, comes and goes every four or five days to and fro between Jamestown and her father's habitation on the great York River. For the heathen were now at peace with us, fearing Smith's strong arm, and the country was as safe and free to us as to themselves.*

Pokahontas, as of old, was in and out with us in these days, watching over us, and bringing us food. She was still the angel of peace ; and when Smith would put in irons some Indian thieves who stole our turkeys, the King Powhatan sends his daughter Pokahontas, who prays Smith to spare the thieves ; whereat he, with sweet looks, and bowing down before her, says it is freely granted, and whatsoever more she asks, " for her sake only."

* This is the statement of the *General History* also.

Now (to put off, for a little time, further *My Cap-tain's great discourse.* discourse of Pokahontas), this Smith was at last the head of all things. I have seen many great and valiant soldiers, but this was the greatest. So brave a spirit dwelt in him, and so great were the ends he had, that no man seeing him could keep from loving him and looking to him as their true leader. He was everywhere, toiling for the good of the colony, and often exclaimed to me (who was his poor friend) what a shame it was the London idlers, with their cards and dice, would not come hither and do men's work for God's honour in the new land.

" Think. Anas !" he saith, walking in the plain called Smithfield, near the palisade, and looking out on the broad river, " who can desire more content, that only hath small means, but only his merits to advance his fortunes, than to tread and plant the ground he hath purchased by his own courage ; planting and building a foundation got from the rude earth by God's blessing, by his own industry, and without prejudice to any ?"

Then his brave face kindles up, and he seems to look far in the future time.

" What so truly suits with honour," he

exclaims, " as the discovering things unknown, erecting towns, peopling countries,
informing the ignorant, reforming things
unjust, and bringing these poor heathen
people to the knowledge of Christ and
humanity ! " *

I would you had seen his face glow as
he thus spake in his brave voice. Certes
there was a look of prophecy in the soldier's eyes, as though he saw somewhat in
the future of this America hid from others ;
and when he speaks the great words
" Christ and humanity " my heart burneth.
Sure (I say to myself), this man belongeth
to the coming time, wherein he looks,
when others will build on his foundation !

For without him this great enterprise
had surely failed and come to nought. He
it was that inspired all hearts, and would
make the sluggards obey and work. Never
was man milder to his old soldiers, but
not to the unruly gallants. He summons
these by beat of drum, and saith to them
sternly : —

" He that will not work shall not eat !
You see now that power resteth wholly
in myself. Therefore he that offendeth,

* The same words may be found in Smith's relation of New England.

let him assuredly expect his due punish- *How Smith dealt with the unruly gallants.*
ment!"

Thereat many murmur, bending fierce
looks on our Captain; but he, growing
ever sterner, and with a harder voice and
look : —

"Dream no longer of this vain hope
that Powhatan will supply corn, nor that
I will longer forbear to force you, or pun-
ish you if you rail! If I find any more
runners off with the Pinnace, let him look
to arrive at the gallows."

He striketh his sword hilt thereupon
and crieth : —

"I protest by that God that made me,
since necessity hath no power to force you
to gather for yourselves, you shall not only
gather for yourselves but for those that
are sick, — they shall not starve!"

With such mild words Smith persuadeth
them, though much against their will;
and they plant corn for the coming har-
vest. He even makes them work at other
work, building a place of retreat against Indian war: the Fort on a ridge above Ware
Creek, which emptieth itself into York
River. We go there with tools, and find a
place on a steep hill hard to approach and
easy to be defended; and hew out brown

stone rock, and build the Place of Retreat, having no mortar. But ere it was finished the want of corn stayed it ; and so we returned to Jamestown.*

So did our worthy Captain rule the tuf-taffty gallants and set 'em to work, with that maxim, "He that will not work, neither shall he eat!" They were hard to rule, but had found one who was their master. Natheless, other things moved the good Captain in these times of trial ; and often I see him go apart, and look out on the river, leaning his face on the hilt of his broadsword. At such times he heaves a sigh, seeming much troubled in his mind ; and looks over his shoulder toward York River, whither he oft would go on this or that business (*with the Emperor*). Once, wandering on the river bank, I see him leaning thus on his sword when, sudden steals up behind him my little Lady Pokahontas, who, coming to the Fort and not finding him there, goes to seek him, and is close to him before he sees her.

Sure never was more gracious image

---

* The " Place of Retreat" here described by Todkill was, it seems, the curious structure called the "Stone House," still standing on Ware Creek not far from York River. It is probably the oldest building in the United States.

(fie! Anas, thou a good Puritan!) than the *The two to-gether.* little maiden of fifteen as she steals up softly to his shoulder. It was spring now, and in place of her robe of down of the wood-pigeon she is clad in a garment woven of the nemminaw grass, which is a close, bright grass wherewith the men weave their stick bucklers. It was wrapped around her shoulders modestly to the chin, and her round neck came out of it, as she looked with laughing eyes over her shoulder, bending her head forward. On her slight arm holding the robe at the throat was a coral bracelet, and a white feather was in her black hair. Even in the woods some fifty yards from her I could see her gracious face and the fond look on it. Sure the swimming eyes fixed on the young soldier were full of an extreme strange tenderness. She touched him and he turned suddenly; whereat I thought he would kiss her, but he did not. His face flushes and he stands looking at her, holding her hands but not speaking a word. Then they walk along the shore, slowly, each beside other; and I hear the low voices mixing with the lap of the waves, but catch nothing.

When they come back to the Fort I see a bright light in my little lady's eyes; and

He goes back with her. the soldier's face glows too, as he looks at her. I know he loves her now, and she loves him, whatever comes of it; since something in the faces of us poor creatures tells our thoughts. 'T was truly a wondrous sight to see this hardy soldier melt, all of a sudden, as the slim form of the girl was there beside him. Her slender shape was like a reed of the river bending in the wind, and her head leaned toward him as the sunflower leaneth to the sun. There were tears in the fawn eyes (I think), but a sudden splendour in the soldier's; and he needs must go a long way with her and her train, through the woods, toward the York.

They went away in that same fashion in the slant sunlight, still looking each at other, and 't was night when he comes back. I meet him by the palisade and say with laughter: —

"Thou art a prisoner at last, worthy Captain!"

At that he muses a little with a flush on the tanned cheeks, and then laughs too.

"Would to heaven I could see *thee*, Anas, in my state!" he says, and leaves me.

Often now, in the after time, I bethink me of those old days at Jamestown, when

these two mortals loved each the other. It *I see all, now.*
was not so strange they should. This great
soldier was comely and gallant, and yet under thirty years ; and my Lady Pokahontas
was nigh fifteen and a woman now. The
Indian girls bloom early, and oft marry in
girlhood ; but had this difference of age
been greater, certes love made them equals,
— him a youth and her a maid that had
come to the time to marry. Howe'er
that be, I know he loved her, this
half-open bell of the woods ;
whereof see in this fur-
ther relation if I
speak the
truth.

IX.

Hawks and Cormorants (so I call Such).

Hawk Argall. SUDDEN the bright days of wandering with Indian maids on river banks, or in the woods, come to an end.

A bruit reaches Jamestown in these spring days, and moves many; it is brought by a trading ship, whereof the commander is a certain Captain Argall, or Captain Buccaneer. He has come cruising about, to traffic with Indians, and fish; but if a merchant ship is seen he is ready to traffic with that too; only he makes such bargain as he will, by talking with cannon, before looking at the flag the barque runs up.

What this Captain Argall says to Smith now when he comes ashore at Jamestown is this:—

"Thou art no longer President of Virginia, worthy Captain. The Company hath removed thee."

"Removed me? Well, for what?" says Smith shortly.

Argall looks at him keenly from under
the bushy eyebrows of his hawk face.

"For hard dealings with the poor Indians, and not sending the ships fraughted."

Thereat Smith bursts out : —

"Hard dealings with Indians!—on the York River, doubtless! I that fed the starving, when this alone was left, am to bear the blame of that!"

"So it seemeth," Argall answers.

"And for not fraughting the ships!—I that told your man Newport to take cedar, not the gilded dirt!"

Hawk Argall thereat laughs, but looks sidewise at Smith's face, I see.

"To the fiend with your Company and all!" cries the soldier, striking his sword hilt. "I like not your look, Master Argall, —beware! Thou art one of these people : shall I tell you what they are? Newport is a talebearer that hath a hundred pounds a year to go to and fro carrying lies. Wingfield is a fat fool, Archer is a mutineer. As to Ratcliffe, he is a counterfeit impostor, whom I've sent home lest my soldiers should cut his throat and so end him!" *

The Captain speaks hotly and Master

---

* These expressions are so similar to Smith's in his *Rude Answer* sent to London as to afford a striking proof of Todkill's accurate memory.

Their talk ends.
Argall says it is time for him to go back to his ship.

"Well, this concerns me not, Captain," he says as he goes, "but what I say is true. My Lord de la Ware is coming as Governor General, with a fleet of ships and half a thousand settlers. By now he has sailed from England, and your friends — I would say these worthies — Newport, Archer, and Ratcliffe are with him. Bend no wrathful looks on me, worthy Captain; I have no part in it. To tell you a secret, I am bent on running a cargo of African negars into Virginia!" *

Thereat he laughs low and departs on his business, not to come back till after times, when he plays a bad game with his hawk face and wary eyes in the Virginia Colony.

Now the day soon cometh when this great Captain Smith will go away from us; but before I tell of that, hear, in few words, what happens to him in this spring, and to the men who built Powhatan his chimney.

One bright morning Smith goes forth to the Glass House, which is in the woods, a

* The cargo was landed by accident in the Bermudas instead of Virginia.

bow-shot or more from the palisade (we are *Smith is at-tacked.*
trying glass there), when sudden he is at-
tacked. A huge Indian leaps on him and
they clutch and fall in the river, where
each would drown the other. But Smith
is too much for him. He throttles him
and drags him ashore, where he would have
struck off his head with his falchion ; but
the Indian begs his mercy. If Smith will
spare him (he says) he will tell who sent
him.

Smith says well, and hears all : it was
the men at Werowocomoco sent to build
the Emperor's house who would make him,
Smith, a prisoner (for some slight), and
yield him up to Powhatan.

While they talk so by signs and some
words, they are at the palisade, where
Smith's old soldiers, hearing all, are in a
great fury.

"I will go cut their throats before the
face of Powhatan!" cries Master George
Percy;* and others say they will go with
him.

But Smith will not, and the Indian gets
off, and the throats are safe, but not their
brains. In the very next year when my

* The same words are attributed to Percy in the *General His-tory.*

Lord la Ware comes as Governor, these same men offer Powhatan to come to Jamestown and make the Lord la Ware his friend.   Thereat the Emperor grunts and ends all in a word.

"You that would betray Captain Smith to *me*," he says, "will surely betray me to this great lord."

With which words he orders their brains to be beat out, which is done ; and so they ended.

Now nought but this is worthy to be set down in my relation of the doings at Jamestown in the spring days of 1609. Hawk Argall sails away, and the place is well rid of him ; and so the days pass on, and the summer blooms, and the August month comes, and with it the English fleet whereof Argall spake.

The English fleet ; but how sorry a sight ! As the ships toil up the great river and come to anchor before Jamestown, they are well-nigh skeleton ships.   For, passing the Azores and sailing westward, a fierce hurricane had struck them ; and we heard how it wracked them, tearing the sails and wrenching the timbers.   One was lost, and the Admiral's ship, the *Sea-Venture*, is driven toward the Isle of Devils and no doubt lost too. A bad business, for on the *Sea-Venture*, with one hundred and fifty men and women, sailed the Lieutenant Governor, Sir Thomas Gates, and the Admiral and the Vice Admiral, Sir George Somers and Captain Newport, with the Letters Patent ; the Lord la Ware remaining in England.

So no new government yet for this ill-starred Virginia ! But certain people coming in the ships mean to see to that. The worn hulks spit out their load of cormorants, — and lo ! here is Ratcliffe and all the old crew. They have been to London whispering to the Company, and blackening Smith and his old soldiers. These would seize the country, divide it, and set up for themselves. Smith is a tyrant who oppresses the poor savages, and will send home no cargoes ; so the Company say the wrong doer shall go.

Ratcliffe comes on shore and boldly says he represents the Governor, and Smith must yield to his authority. Then the evil day comes, and the Fort is torn with factions. To and fro goes Ratcliffe, in and out of the Tavern, drinking deep, and telling the new men Smith is a tyrant and deposed by the Letters in the *Sea-Venture*. More,

Smith's time is nigh expired, and he would seize authority anew ; putting whoso angered him in the stocks or whipping them. So Ratcliffe talks everywhere and therewith forms a faction ; and the days go by hotly (for late summer is come now), and Smith knows not what to do, and exclaims : —

" The London Company will have none of me, and strikes me down, but I will rule these sluggards ! "

It was not a time for love dreams and going to the York River (*to see the Emperor*) now ! Had Smith raised so much as his finger, the Indians, much more his old soldiers, had marched on the rioters ; but he would not. More than once came Pokahontas, and found him ill at ease, knitting his brows and breathing out his passions ; but ever the brows would unknit, and the sweet look come back to him, and he would talk with her in a low voice, looking toward England.

Soon Ratcliffe and the unruly crew thought to openly beard his authority. But it was ill trifling with that lion, who but kept his claws from them for the peace of the Colony. They would take the rule whether or no, saying Smith was no longer

President; and he, putting his clutch on *Ratcliffe's* Ratcliffe, drags him bodily to the Fort, *time.* where he claps him in irons. *end for that*

Thereat all quiets down, and Smith is master of all things. But he is weary and sick at heart, with a great anger and disgust. After all his toils and sufferings for the Virginia Colony, the London people disown him.

"I will no more of them, Anas!" he exclaims to me, striking his sword hilt. "I will put my commission beneath my heel and stamp on it! But first I will go home and face the right honourables with their liar Newport and show the truth. If they listen not, England at least shall hear me!"

X.

I go once more with my Captain to the Place of Retreat.

The two as before. NOW to tell of the last scenes of Smith's stay in Virginia, and his pitiful, brave struggle with the unruly people.

But first of another matter; for ever comes to me the thought, here in my home in Kent in old England, " Thou art writing not of Virginia, Anas, so much as of that blessed Pokahontas! and, though thou tell of other things and people, it behooves thee ever to come back to this angel and discourse of *her*." So now a brief relation of what happeneth at the Place of Retreat on Ware Creek, nigh the York River.

One day of late summer Pokahontas comes to Jamestown, and she and Smith, standing on the platform of the Fort near the cannon, are long in talk. But ever some one comes with this or that he must see to, so that now and again he loseth patience. When the Lady Pokahontas goes away with her wild train in the woods, *Smith would meet somebody.* Smith calls me to him and says : —

"Wilt thou go on a journey with me, Anas ? "

" A journey ? " I say.

" On the morrow. Time presses. Soon I will be gone, and yet I have somewhat to say to somebody. Wilt thou go with me ? "

He spake with a wistful, earnest look and I say : —

" To the world's end. It were little to do for one who hath saved my life in the Transylvania wars. But whither ? "

" Thou shalt see.♦ Now farewell, Anas ; I have work. This cat's-paw Martin hath fled from Nansemunge distraught with fear, leaving his company ; and the men at the Falls are in combustion. Soon I must go thither. To-morrow elsewhere, — and thou with me."

With which he leaves me, and at daylight I feel a hand on my shoulder where I sleep in my hut.

"Rise, Anas !" says a voice, and starting up I behold my Captain in brave apparel girt with his sword.

"Come," he says in earnest tones, " and ask nothing."

Then I follow him, catching up as I go somewhat of bread and meat, for the Tod-kills have ever been keen for provant.

Not a word speaks the Captain as we go out of the palisade where the first light of the sunshine is on the reed thatches of the cabins. None is astir save the guard at the Fort, who salutes the President; and so we push in the woods, and he leads the way toward York River.

Soon I know whither we go. This is the path to the Place of Retreat on the ridge above Ware. We follow it through the forest, wading at times through little streams of water, and hearing the birds sing; when having marched long, we see the laurels and the half-built fort on the wild ridge.

The Captain has said little to me on the way, seeming lost in sorrowful thought. Now he points and says: —

"I shall see her here to-day, Anas."

Thereat his voice sinks low, and he draws a long, deep breath that is piteous to listen to.

"They would still irk me yesterday, and there was no opportunity to have full speech with her," he says in the same voice. "I am going away, and certain

things must be spoken. So she will meet
me here, she says, at this hour to-day.
See, she is coming!"

His face glowed as he spoke, and he
pointed to a light skiff with two in it coming up Ware stream. An Indian youth
was paddling the skiff, and one I knew for
Pokahontas was standing at the prow.

Often now I close my eyes and think of
that sight and of what followed — two people sitting on a stone by the Ware fort with
eyes fixed each on other. I heard nought
that was said and would not, since 't was
not my business. Going apart on the wild
height whereto the approach was only by a
rugged defile amid laurels and evergreens,
I talked by signs with him in the boat, who
was Pokahontas's brother Nantaquaus ; the
manliest, comeliest youth I ever saw for a
savage. I knew not his barbarous lingo,
but natheless saw he was a young prince.
From the first he loved Smith and was
best beloved of the Lady Pokahontas.

The sun was going away to the woods
when the talk of Smith and the maid
ended. He comes to meet us, and clasps
the hand of Nantaquaus and says : —

"We will go, Anas."

Then he turns his head and looks piteously toward Pokahontas, who bends down and weeps. Ere long the maid and her brother have passed to their canoe and are paddling away ; the last we see of her she is bent and seemeth to be weeping still.

Smith looks at the boat till the woods take it and it is no more seen.

" Come Anas," he says in his deep voice, which falters a little, "this hath well-nigh made a child of me."

So we go back to Jamestown, and all the way the worthy Captain speaks no word.

XI.

We lose him whose Loss was our Deaths.

WHAT followeth now is the last that
was seen of Captain Smith in Vir-
inia ; and I, who relate it, make the rela-
on so brief as I can, finding no heart to
ake it other, or dwell at length on it.
  A great sinking at heart and distaste of
ll things had come over Smith.   He was
eary and irate ; all things galled him.
or this man, though the mildest and
weetest to friends and worthy people, was
  lion when aught thwarted him.   He
ould do what was right, not counting
ost to himself ; when others would do the
rong, and brave him — woe to such ! His
eavy wrath and heavier hand would certes
all on them.
  Now, his wrath and grief were great.
he Company had disowned him.   He was
ast away like a worthless husk.   His com-
ission was suppressed he knew not why ;
imself and his old soldiers to be rewarded

The evil day.

he knew not how; and new authority to lie in he knew not whom, — certes it should not lie in Ratcliffe! But the end had come. He could struggle no more; and thereupon he sets all in order, for peace or war, to leave the country.

Little keeps him, and the ships will sail soon. All things are going to confusion. Martin has fled, distraught with fear, from the Company in Nansemunge, and West's people at the Falls are in wild disorder. Smith will see to these and then take himself away. So he draws back the company from Nansemunge, and then for the Falls.

He goes thither in his barge with a picked company, and I go with him. Never saw I man so cool, with so set a purpose in his face. The vain people had begun their plantation at the Falls on marshy ground, and Smith says it shall not be. When they resist and fight, he seizes the leaders and plants the company on the hill of Nonsuch, where Powhatan once had his summer capital.

Then cometh the end. As Smith sails down James River again, a bag of powder explodes in his barge. His clothes catch fire, and he is so tormented by the furious flame he leaps in the river, and scarce his old soldiers drag him into the boat again *A black traitor would murder Smith.* and take him to Jamestown.

Then follows what was burned deep into my memory and still moves me. Smith was lying on his bed tormented by his hurt, and the factions roared around him, and would seek his death where he lay wounded. One traitor comes into his room in the Fort and would murder him ; he puts a pistol to his breast, but Smith, lying still and quiet, looks him steadily in the eye, so that he turns away and durst not. I, Anas Tod-kill, saw this with my eyes and took charge of that traitor, dragging him out by the collar and hurling him against the Fort gate so he reeled, and went away staggering in his gait and muttering.*

As he goes, comes in some one covering her face and shaking with sobs, — my little Lady Pokahontas. But she cannot see him then. He has fainted from his torment, and ere night she goes back weeping with her wild train saying she will return on the morrow. As she went out of the Fort sobbing, she looked up as though to see something that was passing in the clouds, and said, in a low voice, " God !

---

* Ample evidence is to be found in the old relations that Todkill does not exaggerate here. Smith's old soldiers offered, at a sign from him, to cut his adversaries' throats; but he refused to make it.

God ! God !" to my amaze ; and then I knew how in their talks Smith had persuaded her to be a Christian.

All that night I watched by him, and at dawn comes the shot of a culverin : the ships are going back to England, and Smith is firm to go with them. His work is ended in Virginia, if not forever, for this time. The London people will have none of him ; he will tell good-bye to his old soldiers. Captain Percy, a resolute gentleman, is adjudged to act as President, and Smith is carried on board on the backs of his old soldiers, pale and faint. The sailors bustle and make ready the ships ; but an hour before the sailing comes the blessed Pokahontas for a last greeting.

She comes into the cabin where I am standing by Smith, and her sorrowful face lights up the mean place. The month was September, and she was wrapped in a robe of furs, out of which rose the fair flower of her small head, with wan cheeks, woe-begone and moist eyes like the heart's-ease. But I saw there was no heart's-ease in the fair bosom of that maid. Her face streamed with tears, and going to Smith's couch she knelt down and took his thin hand and leaned her wet cheek on it.

Thereat a flush comes to the soldier's face, *My Lady and her soldier say farewell.* and I who had looked on at this strange meeting durst not stay, but went out trembling, leaving them alone, each with other.

Near an hour they were talking together in low words by themselves. Then the culverins roared out giving the signal to weigh anchor, and seeing the ship's Captain going to Smith's cabin I got before him, with fixed intent that no cold eye should pry into this last greeting. I opened the door, and never shall I forget what I there saw. My Lady Pokahontas was kneeling with her arms around him, and his head on her shoulder. Both were pale, and as I came in their lips met in a long kiss. Then the maid turned away from him, hiding her wet face in her fur robe, and with a great sob of farewell went out of the ship and so to shore.

Scarce seeing his face for tears, I myself took my leave of him. With a last grasp of the hand I parted from that true soldier, and, losing him, felt that all things well-nigh went with him. What shall I say of him we thus lost, save that truth and justice were his guides; that he hated sloth and baseness worse than dan-

Our Captain goes away, never to return.

ger and death; that he would send his men nowhere that he would not lead himself; that he would never see us want, and would rather want himself than borrow, or starve than not pay; that he loved action more than words, and hated falsehood more than death; whose adventures were our lives, and whose loss was our deaths.

I looked after the white sails of the ship still they were gone from view toward the wide ocean. Then I come back slow to the dreary palisade, emptied of all joy and satisfaction in my life. When I look around to see where is my Lady Pokahontas she is not there now, but is gone away to her York woods weeping, they say.

XII.

How Master Ratcliffe was a Dead Corpse on the York River.

I, ANAS TODKILL, who write this true The heathen murther us. relation, look back with amaze now on the days that followed in Virginia. Yonder shines the peaceful sunshine on the hop-fields of Kent; my little girl is standing a-tiptoe to pull the spring buds and put in her curls; the black sky and thunder of old days in far Virginia seem a dream to me.

Soon with Smith's going the thunder comes and the lightning too. Losing him we lose all things; yea, his greatest maligners could now curse the evil fate that took him away from us. (God forgive thee, Anas! Didst thou say fate? Nay, 't was Providence, that ordereth all things, and would have us feel the rod for our backslidings.) Sure we feel it now; for the savages no sooner understood our Captain was gone, than all revolted and did spoil and murther all they encountered. It was pitiful; and now see from this what God meaneth when he sendeth a true man to

6

rule. While this Smith stayed with us, the land reposed and the people were fed. The savages would not lift hand in that time, but said each to other, "Smith is coming!" did a stick crackle. But 't was far other now. Nought but blows and arrows and hands imbrued in our blood, when we go to them for succour. All things fall to confusion; the fierce factions fight day and night in the palisade; the people are starving and have no head. Good Master Percy, the new President, cannot hold the reins. He is sick and feeble and would fain go back to England; and the wild horses — so I call the unruly gallants led by Ratcliff — run off, dragging all things after them, till the crash comes.

But far worse than all was the Starving Time that now cometh, whereof my heart shrinks from the relation. To end it ere it begin in earnest, Ratcliffe goes to York River to get corn from Powhatan. I go with him, and what follows is my last sight of the Lady Pokahontas for many a day. Since Smith went she comes no more to Jamestown, and sends nought whereof to eat, in osier baskets or other sort. The old soldiers marvel thereat, and say, Where is the blessed Pokahontas? Why comes she not? But she will not come; to see Ratcliffe's
folly. her once more, I must go to her.

Now this Ratcliffe takes thirty good shot, and would pass over me as one not well affected to him; but I offer, and he says, content, though he scowls at me under his bushy brows. He knoweth well I loved Smith, his enemy, and had certes gone away with him, but for staying behind to nurse my young cousin, Henry Spilman, nigh slain in the fight at Nonsuch. So Ratcliffe says I may go if I will, and turns his back on me, muttering: —

"We want no whining Puritans and psalm - singing rogues for this business! Powhatan's time is come, and the end of him at hand."

"Are you sure of that, good Master Ratcliffe?" I say; whereat he wheels sudden.

"What mean you?" he shouts. "If your Captain Smith could wrest all from him, where were the trouble to do it once more?"

Thereat a wicked smile (I fear) rises to my face, and I would have said, " Thou art other than Smith," but say it not, lest he tell me I shall not go, and so I see not my lady again. I am quiet; and so at dawn of day we set out with the thirty shot, marching through the woods to York River.

What followeth will not fill much time in this my relation. Certes, God had doomed this Ratcliffe, and even the heathens of Greece and Rome said their vain gods first made mad them they would destroy. We come to York River, and Ratcliffe sends one of his men across to the King to ask audience, in a canoe we find there. In an hour comes back the man and saith Powhatan would gladly do so; he loveth the English and would succour them, but *their arms fright his poor people.*

"A snare!" I cry sudden; "he would destroy thee, Master Ratcliffe!"

But he scowls at me and says:—

"Peace! I would have no talk from brawlers!"

"Natheless!"—

"Peace! what would you? I will arrest thee for a brawling knave!"

Whereat I say no more, but listen, and Ratcliffe talks with his people. They say, not go; but he differeth from that. Why not? Since the guns fright the poor people he will leave them and cross as friends. When he says that, I, Anas Todkill, who would not seem faint-hearted, whip my hunting knife in my breast, and hide it there for fear I want it; and then we see

canoes crossing. The King hath sent Cap- *Ratcliffe is slain, and nigh all with him.*
tain Ratcliffe wherewith to come over and
talk with him.

That talk was short. Ratcliffe says he
will go, and every man lays down his arms,
and goes in the canoe, and reaches the
further shore. That was the end.

Sudden the woods swarm with heathen,
and they shout and rush on us, slaying
all that they encounter. Sure never was
bloodier work, and the poor people fell
down dead, pierced with Indian arrows or
beat to death with clubs, holding up hands
over their heads and crying for mercy,
which comes not, sith God has doomed this
Ratcliffe to death, and nigh all them that
came with him.

Now to speak of one Anas Todkill, who
had a knife by good luck, and cut three
heathens with it so that they died ; for I
drave it in them and they fell down with
blood gushing, and hands tearing up grass.
But what was two or three to kill when
many hundreds, nay thousands, more were
there? I say : —

" Thou art dead and gone, Anas ! but remember thou art a Christian and these are
heathens. Sith thou canst not convert
them thou must murther them, lest they
murther thee."

With that I drive at them, hooking my left arm in young Henry Spilman's, and fight through to the woods, and leap a stream to the further bank, where the bushes are close, and fall in the tanglewood. Sudden a voice cries my name, and starting up I see my Lady Pokahontas.

She clasps me close and pulls me deep in the thicket, panting and weeping. Her doeskin robe is all torn by briers, so that her lissom body is near bare, but she heeds it not, nor the boughs catching her black hair, which falleth down to her waist. In her broken English words she crieth there is no time to stay. I must run to the river and swim for my life ; they will soon be on me.

" Then I am dead, Master Todkill," says young Henry, "for I have never yet swum."

"I will not leave thee !" I cry ; " since we have fought together, needs must we die in company."

But the blessed Pokahontas says quick she will save him, and drags him away. But as she doeth so she comes close to me, very pale, and says in a whisper :—

" He is gone, then ? "

I know what she meaneth, and say yes.

Then she turns her head and looks over *I escape to Jamestown.* her shoulder toward England, with wide eyes and tears streaming.

"He will come back some day," she saith low in her Indian tongue. "I know not when, but some day. All is weary, I would go from hence. But do thou go!"

A yell hurries me. The blessed damozel runs off with poor distraught Henry and is hid by the thicket, and I get to York River, and am far from shore swimming lustily ere they see me. Then a race for my life, for canoes come after me with long paddle strokes, and the red heathen stand up yelling, — but they catch me not. Ere their arrows strike me I gain the south shore and plunge in the woods, where I never stop running till I come again to Jamestown.

So ended Captain Ratcliffe and his thirty shot, all but two. That old disturber and mutineer is a dead corpse on the York River, and Master Hamor writ truly his epitaph, that he was "scarce worthy of remembrance but to his dishonour." *

* This account by Todkill of Ratcliffe's death agrees with that in other old relations, where it is stated that only two escaped. "Pokahontas, the King's daughter," says another narrative, "saved a boy called Henry Spilman that lived many yeeres after, by her meanes, amongst the Patawomekes." Todkill's is the only full account of the expedition.

XIII.

We go through the Wilderness to the Land of Canaan.

The Starving Time. NOW see what that meaneth; we all found the want of Captain Smith, yea his greatest maligners could now curse his loss. This poor dead Ratcliffe ever irked him, saying *he* was the true leader, not Smith; and yet behold how Providence fashioneth things. These two men tried the same business of getting corn from Powhatan; and one was fooled and got none, only his death, when the other (Smith) got the corn and his life too.

But it were idle to speak more hereof. The woful *Starving Time* is coming now. Who can tell of it without sighs and tears, and the conclusion making God's mercy manifest! Now there was no more corn, and men died of mere famine, looking with dumb amaze each in other's eyes. When we went to the Paspaheghs praying succour, we had nothing for our pains but mortal wounds with clubs and arrows. At last

all was eaten, hogs, sheep, and horses, and
what lived, — nought was spared. Acorns,
walnuts, and berries, and a few fish, was
now all; we did eat the skins of horses,
and at last one another. We slew a savage
and buried him, but the poorer sort did dig
him up and eat him; and so did divers
one another boiled and stewed with roots
and herbs. Yea, *one did kill his wife*, and
had eat part of her, ere we knew it, for
which we burned him, as he well deserved,
heaping fagots around that wretch tied to
a stake in the street at Jamestown, and seeing him burn, with loud yells, till he died
for his foul murther of his innocent wife.

How a man did eat his wife and we burned him.

This was that time which still to this
day we call the Starving Time. Oh, the
horror of it! Even now it comes back to
me in a sudden quaking. Of five hundred
men, women, and children scarce sixty were
now alive, and they poor miserable creatures that prayed for death to end their
sufferings. 'T was the bright May month,
but the sunshine brought us no joy. Not
one hour passed but some dead body was
trailed out to be buried by them that nigh
fell in the grave with the dead, for feeble-
ness. By the palisade all were huddled
together; men, women, and children, white

and ghostlike, with yearning eyes looking to England. The strong men (once) would gnaw wood and the grass blades; and it was pitiful to see the mothers hugging babes close to dry bosoms, praying God to send them milk.

Sudden, one day, I hear a cry and run out of the Fort (staggering a little, I think).

"A sail! a sail!" the babbling voices say; and the crowd totters to the shore.

"Blessed be God for all his mercy to his creatures!" I say, lifting up my eyes; for there was a sail coming up the river; nay, two, white against the fringe of woods.

The foremost was the cedar ship, built by brave Admiral Somers in the Bermuda Islands, whereon the *Sea-Venture* had been shipwrecked the year before. This was the *Deliverance* (for which deliverance God be thanked!); and the other was the *Patience*, built with bolts from the wrecked *Sea-Venture*.

So the white sails slowly come, and in the midst of a babbling crowd lands the Admiral Sir George Somers, and Sir Thomas Gates, the Lieutenant Governor, and looks around them. Oh, the dreary sight! The Jamestown place was a wreck. The cabins were nigh gone for firewood, and the palisade half torn down. The gates swung on *We sail for England.* broken hinges, and the Fort platform scarce held up the cannon.

Admiral Somers, landing first, puts his chin in his hand and looks on with tears. The poor people crowd round him crying, "Bread! bread!" whereat a great sob shakes him, and he gives orders to his sailors, who haste to the ship to bring it. Soon the crowd is fed, and then they jostle and babble and cry with one voice, "England! England!" most of all the mothers, and the Admiral says they shall go. In his ships he has but fourteen days' provisions, but he will try. No, he will not desert us; as God sees him he will succour us. All shall embark quick, and a day is fixed and all is ready.

The sight was piteous, to see these wretches crowd on the ships, half crazed with joy, and nigh out of their heads. They would have burned the cursed place that they could nevermore return to it; but God, who would not have this fine country unplanted by Englishmen, put it into the heart of the Admiral Somers to forbid that. Having buried the cannon at the gate of the Fort, he posts a guard on the palisade and hurries the poor people aboard. The drum rolls for the signal and all are shipped, and the Admiral follows. A salute is fired then as the ships move, — farewell to Jamestown!

But said I not that God would not have this land of Virginia fall back in heathenesse? Blessed be his name for all his goodness; for when the ships stopped a night at Mulberry Isle, here comes at dawn a swift barge shooting up the river, flying the English pennon. Thereat a great shout rises and cries of amaze, — what is coming? It is my Lord la Ware, with more ships and Englishmen. He hath stopped a little below, but hearing Jamestown is abandoned sendeth his orders to go back there and await him; so we go back joyfully.

Next day comes this brave Lord la Ware in his ships, with flags flying, and lands on shore, and kneels down, with shut eyes, and prays for a season; glad at heart he comes in time to save Virginia. Then the drums roll loud once more, and the church is open for service, and all is joy in the Virginia plantation, which was dead and is alive again.

Writing here in the after days, I, Anas Todkill, shut my eyes as my Lord la Ware shut his, and see all that once more. Sure *The arm of the Lord of Hosts.* 't was God's infinite providence ; and needs must his poor people cast themselves at his very footstool and adore his goodness. For had he not sent Sir George Somers from the Bermudas, within four days we had famished ; and if we had set sail sooner and launched on the vast ocean, how encounter the fleet of the Lord la Ware? This was the arm of the Lord of Hosts, who would have his people pass the Red Sea and wilderness, and then to possess the land of *Canaan*. So I say with the heathen Socrates, " If God for man be careful, why should man be over distrust-ful?"

XIV.

How Some One did break a Poor Man on the Wheel.

The Lord la Ware.

AS I go back in memory, and all these old times come to me, ever I think, "Thou didst set out, Anas, to discourse of the Lady Pokahontas only. Who art thou to write histories, whereof thy betters can scarce make aught but lying repertories nothing worth?"

So, soon, we will come back to that blessed damozel. But some strange things happed before, whereof I needs must write this brief relation, though some discredit that bloody marvel of which I was told. Was it the High Marshal Dale that did it, or some other? Whoever he be, he must answer before the judgment.

Now, not to tarry long or discourse of my Lord la Ware in Virginia. He was a brave and great lord, soft of heart, and did much for us. He stays from spring to spring only, and builds forts and feeds his people; but for more supplies sends

Sir George Somers, the old Admiral, in his cedar ship to the Bermudas, where is much fruit and other, with wild hogs left there by the Spaniard. So the Admiral sails forth to the Isle of Devils, not to return. When he comes there and loads his ship with pomegranates and such tropic stuff, he falls sick, when he entreats his men, like a valiant Captain, to be constant to their duty and go back to Virginia. Then he dies, but they, as men amazed, seeing the death of him who was the life of them all, embalmed his body and sailed for England. Sure that was a traitorous act, but they returned not to Virginia. The cedar ship, with his dead body, arrived at White Church, in Dorset, where by his friends he was buried, with volleys of shot and the rites of a soldier. So he ended, this brave Admiral, that saved us at Jamestown.

Now not much more of his great lordship, my Lord la Ware, who kept royal state. He would still go to church with his Lieutenant Governor and High Admiral and Master of the Horse and all his brave company, followed by fifty halberd-bearers in scarlet cloaks. There he sits himself in a velvet chair, with a silk cushion to kneel on, after the vain Church of England fashion; and the church is fitted with cedar pews and a walnut table and font, and hath two bells at the west end; the whole some sixty feet long. I, Anas Todkill, would go oft, though my Puritan heart liked not all this mummery, least of all *the flowers* wherewith my Lord la Ware would still deck his church. These papists' abominations made my heart to burn; and oft looking at the walls, chancel, and pulpit nigh covered with red and white roses, I say to myself: —

"Away! thou relics of a vain worship! thou temptations of the Evil One!"

And what irketh me most of all is that these Church of England Virginians, or as the new term hath it Episcopalians, have nought to say against them. Even they love these snares of Satan, and one says, laughing, to me when I grumble: —

"Why not dress the church with flowers, Master Todkill? Sure 't is innocent, sith God made them; and if the Good Book saith 'all shall worship Him,' why not the flowers?"

With which vain talk they would think to persuade Anas Todkill, a good Puritan, but cannot!

When my Lord la Ware falls sick and goes to England in early summer, comes the High Marshal, Sir Thomas Dale, a stalwart ruler. Soon his heavy hand falls on the unruly gallants, who will not work, and play bowls in the grass-grown streets of Jamestown.*

He is the master of the gallants quick : they shall work, and not be fed like drones by the working bees. He is right in that, but soon the valiant High Marshal shows his claws in far other matters. He would have his way in all, and the old soldiers like not that. Brief, he brings from England his "Code Martial and Moral," writ by Master Strachey, whereby he can do aught he will ; and when this pleases few, and a company say this martial law is a thing unlawful, whereof I, Anas Todkill, was one, comes a fierce and bloody business. Jeffrey Abbot and other of Smith's old soldiers are arrested, and the Marshal shoots most all, and tortures many.† Some

---

* The writer fails to mention that Sir Thomas Gates, the Lieutenant Governor, had been sent to England, and that Percy, who was left in charge of the colony, could not rule the "gallants." In writing many years afterwards these details may have escaped his memory.

† It is necessary in reading this account to remember that Todkill by his own confession was one of the conspirators, and that his statements are to be taken cautiously. The conspiracy probably aimed

7

His cruel and barbarous act.

have awls thrust through their tongues, others are tied by the thumbs and hoisted from the floor, and one was *broke on the wheel.*

I who write saw not this, for it took place inside the Fort, whereof a guard at the door stopped all who would enter. But Jeffrey Abbot told me that Barebones Prym told him that Praise-the-Lord Wilkins told him that he heard 't was done to one whose name was hid. This was the foul and unnatural way of it. The man was stretched on a frame, and four horses chained to his arms and legs, and men with whips ready. Would he confess and tell his accomplices? If he would, then his life should be spared; but he had nought to do with the business, he cried.

At that, one standing by crieth:—

"Whip! he shall tell!"

Whereon the horses are whipped up and his legs and arms are pulled and the bones crack. The man faints, but comes to, and is asked again if he will confess. He moans he cannot, having nought to tell. Then the voice cries once more:—

"Whip! the wretch shall own all!"

at much more serious ends than a simple protest against the enforcement of martial law. The deposition or death of Dale seems to have been contemplated by the leaders, though probably not by Todkill.

The horses start and drag him nigh *Who told me* asunder, and his leg-bones start out, with *thereof.* gushes of blood. The poor wretch crieth shrill, " Kill me ! " but the blood in his throat stops him. Then the man standing by — I wot not who he was, I think not the Marshal — says to one : —

" Sith he would die, let it be so, as the law directs."

And this one who is spoke to lifts a club wherewith he is furnished, and breaks the bones of the poor wretch on the frame ; and, last, dashes his brains out and so ends him.

For this I vouch not, hàving not seen it ; and scarce I think the valiant Marshal, who was stern but not pitiless, ever ordered it ; natheless 't is here related. Jeffrey Abbot, Smith's old sergeant, a true man too, told me he heard it. Barebones Prym told him that Praise-the-Lord Wilkins told him that 't was done, or another told him he heard 't was done. If so be, the Lord doubtless will requite them that did it ; for the right lieth in none to put men to death by so barbarous, unusual, and cruel punishment.* Natheless, for a last

---

* There is no doubt that men were broken on the wheel at this period in Virginia. One account speaks of the " cruel, painful, and unusual " punishments inflicted ; another states that the manner

Argall drives the French people from Mount Desert.

word, I cannot believe the Marshal ordered it ; it may be 't was done by Argall, that hawk-buccaneer who brought the ill news to Smith, and was now back in Virginia seeking something to pounce on. But I know not.

Now this same Argall is sent on a buccaneer business to kill innocent people before he seizes my Lady Pokahontas, as my relation will show. News comes to Jamestown that the French are settling on Virginia ground in Nova Scotia, at Mount Desert Island, and Dale sends Argall to rout 'em out. Which he does without word, shooting men and women down there at this Mount Desert, whereof I know not ; and thence sails to the Hudson River and drags down the Dutch flag at Albany Fort and Manhattan Island in Virginia. So he comes back in triumph, this hawk and buccaneer, and next seizes my Lady Pokahontas and brings her to Jamestown.

was one customary "in France;" and certain Virginia Burgesses of 1624 deposed that to their personal knowledge men had been put to death "by hanging, shooting, *breaking on the wheel, and the like.*"

XV.

How my Lady Pokahontas is brought to Jamestown a Prisoner.

THE treacherous betrayal, to call it by its right name, of my Lady Pokahontas, takes place in this wise. But first of the strangeness of my lady never visiting us again after Smith goes.

How she went away after that last leave-taking this true relation hath shown; and how I, Anas Todkill, saw her but once only thereafter, when again she saved my poor life. But never she comes to Jamestown any more now, and seemeth as one dead to us. In old days (as hath been told) she was ever in and out with her wild train (and baskets), but now no Pokahontas and no wild train; worse than all, no baskets! She cometh not, and, as we hear, is not now at Werowocomoco. Some say she and the Emperor have quarrelled; others that she hath made a princely progress for her divertisement to the country of Potowamak. Only, I find after this, from some broken words she herself speaketh, that she cannot bear the scenes where she and Smith were together, and goes away to dull her grief.*

What is most to us, she comes no more ; and after a while the English think her to be dead; but sudden we hear of her and see her too, which happened as followeth.

This same Captain Argall, the hawk, going to the river Potowamak for corn, whereof he would fain bring back a ship full, is told by Japazaws, an Indian chief there, that the Lady Pokahontas is with him. Thereat Argall, much marvelling, and most to hear she is in hiding, as they said, bargains with Japazaws to buy her for a copper kettle, to which he agrees. Now see the treacherous falsehood of these savage people, who would betray their very guests even for what they covet, valuing like girls the giddy pleasure of the eyes beyond faith and honour. Japazaws his wife is foremost in this bad business, and wileth Pokahontas on board the ship, where there

---

* This passage clears up an obscure question. Raphe Hamor says, that "the Nonparella of Virginia," as he calls Pokahontas, made "a princely progress," to see her people on the Potomac; and another writer describes her as residing there and "thinking herself unknown."

will be a fine banquet, she saith. So Poka- *And brought a prisoner to Jamestown.*
hontas goes, and is betrayed to Argall ;
and for all her weeping and entreaties is
carried back a prisoner to Jamestown ;
there to be held as a hostage for the good
behaviour of her father the Emperor.

Never saw I so sad a face as when she
landed from the ship and stepped into the
Fort. She was ever looking around her
at this and that she remembered, weeping
the while ; and, most, I could see her eyes
bent on the casements of that room wherein Smith lay when he was ill. Her face
streamed with tears, and great sobs shook
her body ; and I, gazing at her, was in
amaze at her gracious beauty. She was
now some eighteen years, and a full woman, though slight of stature. The maid
had grown a princess, with great dark eyes,
soft and clear, and a frame slim but round,
and swaying as she walked on her small
feet. She was wrapped in a feathered
robe, and passed proudly through the
throng scarce looking at any one. Sudden
she catches sight of me and stops, and
coming to me, takes my two hands, and
bursts into weeping as her heart would
break. Then she goes in the Fort ; the
gate is shut : and my little Lady is to be

Smith is dead, they say.

held a prisoner till Powhatan send back some men and muskets taken from the Colony.

It would be long to relate how I came to be my lady's henchman, going her errands and waiting on her, as a father waits on his child for loving her; so it happed. She had her room in the Fort, and an English maid, but ever when she would talk with any one she sent for Anas. Never was talk so sorrowful as mine with my Lady Pokahontas in these days. The bruit had come that Smith was dead, and when she hears it, a great sob shakes her, and she bends down moaning most like a poor bird that is shot and bleeding. How and where had he died? but we know nothing. In a sea-fight off the Azores, some said, and some another story. But none denied he was gone, and his old soldiers wept for him; I more than all, remembering that true-hearted soldier who had been so dearly beloved of me. So we cried together like children,— poor Anas Todkill and the little princess. She talked long of the young soldier, and had a legion of old stories of him. But ever she fell again to weeping, and saying in a low voice as before, when she took leave of him, "God!

God!" whereby I knew she was still a Christian and faithful to her vows.

The time passed, and at length this first outburst of a heavy heart gave way to quiet. She wept no more, as the days went on, but would move about softly, thinking and sometimes talking lowly to herself. When she passed me at such times, she would raise her head and smile pitifully, and lay her little hand on my doublet and say, "Good Anas!" which pleased me much. They let her go out of the Fort whither she would, so she went not away ; and one day I followed her and saw her stand on the shore, at nigh sunset, where Smith had been standing when she stole up behind him. When she came back to the Fort she was weeping.

But time is a hard enemy, and the grave an ill remembrancer. Oh, lamentable ! we pass away, and those we best loved turn otherwhere. Is it God's great mercy that sends this oblivion to his poor creatures ? Certes it must be so, since all human things flow from Him. So my lady grows quiet and her sorrow settles down in her heart, I think. She even laughs a little at times, and being a girl, which is a thoughtless creature, takes part in the games of the young men and maids, whereof there are plenty now. The youths (and the older men for that) would much affect her company, for she had a fine mirth and an extraordinary sweet smile, with a love of what was humourous that made her wondrous pleasant.

So my little lady laughed, and, as the wont of her vain sex is, looked at the gallants with side glances out of the corners of her black eyes. But ever under this fooling was plain to me the old, settled sorrow, and the mourning deep down in her heart for the soldier she had loved, and who had loved her, and was dead now. Master Shakespeare (I thought) writes plays, taking his stories from books; methinks he should be here now, and see this woman's heart moaning over a dead love, — and dreaming of a new.

XVI.

I make Acquaintance of Master Rolfe.

NOW to go on with this true relation, and tell what in due time followed. *Master Rolfe loves my Lady.*
My Lady Pokahontas (as I still would call her) had much converse on holy things with the valiant and religious High Marshal, Sir Thomas Dale, Governor General; and but for being converted, he would certes have converted her. For the gaining of that one soul (he said), he would think his time and toil in Virginia well spent;* but this relation showeth that ere now she was a Christian.

Natheless she was young and mirthful, and affected company, and others affected her. Now among them was a worthy gentleman, some thirty, Master John Rolfe. For all his youth he was a grave, staid man, much given to religious exercises, and I first surmised his thought as to Pokahontas by his making friends with me.

---

* Sir Thomas Dale makes this declaration in a letter to a friend in London.

I talk with him.

He would still salute me as he passed into the Fort with a bow, and "A pleasant morn, Master Todkill," or "Give you good-day, friend." Thereat I marvelled and was pleased, for Master Rolfe was high in the Governor's graces ; but one day when we were alone together, I came to know his mind, and why he thus affected me.

"You were one of Captain Smith's old soldiers, were you not, Master Todkill ? " he asked of me. Whereupon I answered Yes, for I had fought under him against the Turk.

"And in Virginia also," he goes on in his grave, friendly voice. "I know the true story of old times here, and what manner of man Smith was. He is dead now, God rest him ; but we build on his foundation."

At this my heart warmed, and I spoke to Master Rolfe of the old days, giving my dear and noble Captain the character was his due.

"A mighty soldier, and dwarfs us all," answered Master Rolfe. "My own life, I think, is nothing beside his with his brave adventures and great deeds."

Thereat, musing, he speaks of himself and says : —

"I was married early in England, Master Todkill, and brought my young wife in the fleet under the good Admiral Somers, seeking Virginia. But God would not have it that she should ever see this virgin land. We were on board the *Sea-Venture,* and that was wrecked on the Bermudas. There my dear wife died, after giving birth to her babe, a girl. I called the little cherub sent me, *Bermuda,* after the islands, but she died too, and both rest there, and I am alone, Master Todkill."

This moved me much, and the talk there ended ; but soon I saw that this so great wound in the heart of Master Rolfe was well-nigh healed, for he had begun to love my little Lady Pokahontas. Thereat my heart burned within me. Did my Lady Pokahontas love *him ?* That were piteous, after Smith ; and a great anger suddenly seizes me, most at this Master Rolfe, who would steal from my dear Captain this heart that belonged to him. Even now was this bruit true that Smith was dead ? (I said this to myself,) and was Master Rolfe the one who had got it believed in the Colony ?

So the next time he meets me and would talk of my Lady, I greet him but

The strife in his thoughts. coldly, and am silent. Thereat he looks strangely at me, as though in sudden pain, and heaves a great sigh.

"You would hold no speech with me, then, worthy Master Todkill?" he says lowly. "I know your thought. That great soldier was your friend and loved this maid; therefore you would not have her love me, or I her, I see. Certes 't is a great sin; I grant you that; but not to your sometime Captain. He is dead, they say; think you he is not?"

"The bruit saith so," I answer short, "but I know not whence it comes or who hath spread it."

"Not I!" cries Master Rolfe. "Would to God that true soldier were alive for the honour of England!"

"Say you so?" I answered; "are you honest?"

"I swear I am honest, Master Todkill. I think him verily to be dead in a combat off the Azores, and 't is no sin in me to love her."

"And yet you said 't was a great sin."

"Certes, in that the Scripture forbids a Christian man to marry a strange wo-man."

Then sudden I see his mind, and being

a Puritan, and not a mere court ruffler, *He sees my Lady in his sleep.* think well of this man whose conscience hurts him in such a matter.

"Say you that?" I answer. "You love her, and yet hold back?"

Thereat his face colours up, and he says in a loud voice, careless who hears him from the Fort, —

"Love her? God knoweth I love her with my heart and soul! Scarce I sleep for thinking of her, and yet I know not if she thinketh of me, nor if I would have her think of me."

I listen, but say nothing, looking intent at his face.

"This gracious creature," he saith at length, "hath made a mighty war in my meditations. Long I have struggled, Master Todkill, remembering the displeasure God conceived against the sons of Levi and Israel for marrying strange wives. Doubtless, I said, this is the enemy that seeketh man's destruction, and so rested. But then when I had obtained my peace behold another gracious tentation hath made a breach in my meditations. I see her in my sleep, and awake to astonishment. I am pulled here and there, as it were, and a voice crieth, 'Why do not thou

marry her and endeavour to make her a
Christian ? ' "

. " Know you not she is such now ? " I
say.

" Yes, Master Todkill; my poor speech
wanders ; I would confirm her in such holy
thoughts, for God's honour and the good
of the Colony."

Such' honesty spoke in his voice that I,
looking at him, grew not so cold to him.
This he doubtless sees, and says in earnest
words : —

"Certes the vulgar sort, who square all
men's actions by their own evil thoughts,
will jeer at me, Master Todkill, and say I
am only moved by carnal longing ; but
God, who seeth me, knoweth otherwise.   I
would marry this gracious maiden for his
glory and the good of his people.   I have
made all known to Him in my daily, yea
hourly, prayers and meditations ; and sure
I think He doth approve it.   Think what
good will surely come!   Think how beautiful is the soul of this creature Pokahontas ; of her desire to be taught and instructed in the knowledge of God ; her
capableness of understanding ; her aptness
and willingness to receive any good im-
pression ; and I deny not besides this spir-

itual, her own incitements stirring me up
hereunto ! " *

He stops all in a tremble, and saith : —

"What I do is for God's glory, as God
seeth me ! "

We had walked to the river shore, and
the tide coming in lapped on the bank, as
that day when Smith was looking, and my
Lady stole to him.

For all the voice of Master Rolfe was
honest and full of a strange trouble, I still
was obstinate and could not bring me to
believe in him.

"Sure what you say is worthy of a true
man and a Christian," I say ; "but natheless in such things there is more : the
consent of the maiden.   Howe'er a man's
thought be torn whether or no he will wed
such an one, there remains to know this :
whether such an one will wed *him*."

Thereat his head drooped down.   He
studied for a time, and answered : —

"I know not.   I scarce dare hope that,
after Smith, she will cast eyes on *me*.
But think, Master Todkill ; he is dead, as
I verily believe ; and what better can the
gracious creature do than bethink her that

---

* What Rolfe said in this interview is identical with what he wrote
in the letter spoken of by Todkill a little further on.

8

He will ask counsel. one loves her that still liveth and will cherish her ? "

That was hard to gainsay, and Master Rolfe had hit it. Doubtless many bleeding hearts have had this to choose: whether the past time shall be buried and the old love forgot, or not, for a new love that offereth. But I could not bear to think of it, that my dear Captain should be thus forgotten.

"What shall I do, Master Todkill?" Master Rolfe saith sudden; but I shake my head.

"I know not; seek other to advise you, Master Rolfe," I answer.

Thereat he heaves another sigh and says : —

"Yes ; I will tell all in a letter to my worthy friend, Sir Thomas Dale. He is a valiant and religious man, well instructed in divinity, which be rare in a martial man.* He shall decide."

Wherewith we go back silent, with the waves still lapping, to the Fort.

---

* Rolfe here borrows an expression which he had no doubt heard employed by the Rev. Alexander Whitaker, Minister of the Varina parish, and called the "Apostle of Virginia." He uses it in a letter to a friend in London.

XVII.

*I think, Sure 't is better to be off with the
Old Love ere on with the New.*

SOON Master Rolfe writes that letter Master Rolfe's letter. in which he would ask Sir Thomas his consent. I know this from accident. Chancing to pass him while he is walking by the palisade with Master Raphe Hamor, Secretary of the Colony, I must needs overhear him (though I would not) say these words :—

"'T is written, friend Raphe ; I ask him what shall I do ? My whole heart is therein, and thou shalt give it him, when thou wilt."

With that he holds out a letter and Master Hamor takes it, smiling, and they pass. The opportunity to deliver the letter came soon, and I was witness of all ; but first some words of my dear Lady Pokahontas. It was ill for me being wroth with her, since only my own misery followed. And there was nought really to make me so. Sure not the least thing was to her dishonour. This noble princess was yet faithful to one that had loved her, though he were dead. The old wound was yet sore and would not heal up in that time.

But, welladay! ever the time went on; and the spring ripened to summer; and then the summer to what in this land we call, after Indian fashion, the Leaf-Fall; and ever with the passing days the heart of my Lady taketh more ease, and her face smiles with a brighter light in it. But when some one let fall *his* name, sudden tears would come and she would go away sorrowful by herself; and ever when she comes back she lays her hand softly on me, looking me in the face as though to say, " *We* remember, Anas."

At such times comes Master Rolfe and sits beside her and talks to her, though she seems not willing. Long before this she was mistress of English, and spoke it freely, in her old lisping voice, very low, but exceeding sweet. And ever as she lisped out her words, I could see the face of Master Rolfe flush up as he listened to her. Would she ever love him, and what good would come of that letter to Sir Thomas? (I said.) 'T were a brave jest indeed to know if he should marry a maid *Her faith in unfaith.* who would not!* Whether his wooing prospered I could not tell from looking at my little Lady.   Certes she would smile on him at times, but the smile was sorrowful; and if she bent her head sidewise, looking at him over her shoulder, after the wicked wont of maids, soon she looked down and sighed grievously, doubtless remembering.

Sooth to say, Master Rolfe was not so strange to love her.   She was now clad like an English woman, in some clothes they had given her, and would deck herself carefully in ruff and stomacher, and spend much time on her hair at back of her head, seeking to make it curl, and put it in a cushion, after the fashion of the time.   On her feet were Spanish shoes of green morocco, with high red heels, showing her wondrous small feet, with clocked stockings on the ankles.   Her round arms were ever naked, with coral bracelets on her wrists; and as she moved, the slim figure of the maid was like a willow-tree, such as groweth on the Virginia rivers. Sure 't was a beauteous vision, with the brown face bent forward, and a smile on

* Todkill's meaning here seems to be that it was rather comic for Rolfe to have scruples as to marrying one who would not marry him.

the lips and in the eyes ; and looking at her, Master Rolfe would heave a piteous sigh, whereat she must needs laugh.

But a man's true love for a woman is strong. Much as my little Lady would laugh, I could at length see she was giving way. They often walked to the shore together and came back with heads bent down ; and now, I think, she did not so much affect my company as before. Often she would look at me in a sad, doubtful way, as though to say, "An I were to, Anas?" But never had she speech with me save on other things ; never on this one.

So the winter passed away, and the spring was near, and then I came to know what would be. One day toward April I was wandering in the woods, when the sound of voices comes to me from a path through the thicket, and these two, my Lady and Master Rolfe, pass near me. Her head is leaned down and her face is red with blushes; and Master Rolfe is talking to her low and earnest as they go by. He stops speaking as they come near, and for a little time she makes no answer. Then I hear only these words from her, like the whisper of the south wind in the leaves, "Do you really ?"

They passed on, thereupon, but I could *My Captain is forgot.* see Master Rolfe take her hand that was hanging down at her side and press it in both his, and kiss it. Would she take it away? I waited, with my heart beating. She let him hold it in his own, and looked up over her shoulder into his eyes that were fixed on her.

Then I knew that my dear Captain was forgot at last.

XVIII.

We sail up York River with my Lady, and what followeth.

*Master Rolfe
hath a quiet
conscience
now.*CERTES comes to my poor heart a
great throbbing as I go back to the
Fort. This was the end; my little Lady
had forgot her Captain. I would scarce go
near her, and she understands that, for she
looks at me with such tears as her heart
would break; and for nigh a week would
scarce speak so much as a word to Master
Rolfe.

But maidens are ever changeful. 'T is
at most an April day with such. The rain
goes, and the shine comes back after the
shower, and they are brighter than before. Soon poor Anas is clean forgot, and
when they encounter, my little Lady seems
ashamed to meet his eyes.

Now to tell what followed. Had Master
Rolfe determined in his mind that his conscience should be quiet as to marrying
strange wives? Once he saith it is against

Scripture, and sure this Lady Pokahontas *He would* *embrace his* belonged to a cursed generation. Now the *fair Satan.* generation appeareth not so cursed, rather blessed, and to be gladly wed with! Where be now the *perturbations of his distracted soul* (as he saith), and those same snares of the Evil One set in the black eyes of the maid? When he dreameth of her (if one would hear him), he starts from sleep and cries, "Get thee behind me, Satan!" But natheless he would embrace this fair Satan, and make her his Devil's-helpmate! and the witch herself is willing, and will have Master Rolfe to husband.

All growling, you will say, of poor Anas Todkill at his Captain's being so soon forgot, and at him who supplants him: this Master Rolfe, who would not *wed with strange wives*, but hath got the better of that, and remembers that *they that turn souls to righteousness shall shine as the stars forever!* (Natheless *this one* was turned already, and needed him not.) Again thou growlest, Anas! So be it; men will growl considering love's wiling, and the doings of these farthingales who make us love 'em. Not that my little Lady did not yet love the soldier she had loved so in old days. She loved him deep in her heart of hearts, far more, I think, than this new love. But the old lover was dead, you see, and Master Rolfe pressed strong. He had friends, too, that spoke for him : Master Strachey, he that writ the " True Repertory of the Wrack and Redemption of the Sea-Venture," a civil-spoken gentleman ; and also Master Raphe Hamor, who took the letter for Sir Thomas Dale, to ask his counsel.

Now I will relate how this letter was delivered and what strange matter followeth.

To go back: when Powhatan hears his daughter is taken a prisoner and carried to Jamestown he is bitter offended, and keepeth silence; when messengers go to him from Sir Thomas and say the Lady Pokahontas shall be sent back when certain Englishmen, who are captives, with their muskets, are given up to us, Powhatan will not, and still keeps quiet. Thereon Sir Thomas bethinks him he will go and take 'em, and in the March days of this year 1613 sails with picked men in a ship by Point Comfort into York River, and so to Werowocomoco. He takes my Lady Pokahontas with him, and in the ship goeth also Master John Rolfe, who is a worshipful gentleman and high in his honour's favour. My lady is sad and smiling

by turns on the way, Sir Thomas his in- *We land at Machot.*
tent being to surrender her when the arms
are brought with the English prisoners by
Powhatan.

At Werowocomoco was no Powhatan,
but a great multitude of Indians on the
bank of the river, who jeered loud as we
came near shore, and with scornful bravado
affronted us, demanding, "Why come you
hither? You are welcome if you come to
fight; we will use you as we used Captain
Ratcliffe." Then they let fly their arrows,
at which we manned boats and went
ashore. There we burned all their houses
and spoiled all they had; and going to
ship again sailed up the river.

Now to tell what next happed, and how
the mind of my little Lady was at last
known to all. We got to Machot, Opechancanough's capital city, where the York
River divideth,* and went ashore in a
great crowd, sending to Powhatan who was
in the woods, to tell our minds. We had
brought Pokahontas, and would deliver her
whenas the arms were brought; and Master John Rolfe and one more were sent on
this errand. They went with guides to the

* The present West Point, at the confluence of the Pamunkey and
Mattapony.

Emperor's woods palace, but he not choosing to see them (of his grim humour) sent back a vain message as all would be well; but no further.

At this Sir Thomas Dale concludes the Emperor but trifles with him, and is about giving orders to lay waste all houses and boats and the very fish weirs, when sudden happens what stops all. To make this plain: my Lady Pokahontas, in a brave gown, and looking very proud, had come ashore with the rest. Scarce she spoke to any of her people, only to say to the better sort with a proud and hurt voice:—

"If my father loved me he would not value me less than old swords, pieces, or axes; so I will still dwell with the Englishmen, who love me."

Thereat she turned her head a little and looked at Master Rolfe, who smiled as approving, and signed with his hand to her, and to Master Raphe Hamor, who was standing near. Then I see this Master Hamor go to Sir Thomas and give him a letter, and I know in my heart it is Master Rolfe's letter about the marriage, asking Sir Thomas his consent, and what ought he to do. When Sir Thomas Dale opens the folds of paper he looketh a little puzzled at first; then he turns to the end to see by whom 't is writ. Seeing there, doubtless, Master Rolfe's name, he looketh toward him, but he is in some confusion; and chancing to behold the Lady Pokahontas at this same minute, I see she is blushing red and hanging down her head.

Sir Thomas goes back and peruses the letter with a grave look: but soon his face lights up and, holding back his head with his beard in the air, he laughs loud.

" Ho, ho!" he says, turning to Master Rolfe; " thou art a sly one! What is this? never you said a word of it, though we were oft together, Master Rolfe."

" I durst not," says Rolfe all of a tremble. "I feared thou wouldst say nay, good Sir Thomas."

" So you held all back!"

" Yea, Sir Thomas, till this moment. But now you needs must know, since you would burn all, and destroy these poor people that are " —

" Madame Rolfe's kindred!" cries Sir Thomas, laughing loud and looking from him to Pokahontas. Thereat she blushes, but suddenly starts and goes forward very quick. Her brother Nantaquaus pushes

Nantaquaus. through the crowd and catches her close to his breast and kisses her. Never saw I faces shine so, and they babble and kiss and she tells him all; for a great wonder comes to his face, the comeliest I ever saw in a savage.

"Would you? would you?" he says, having a few English words. Whereto Pokahontas laughs, and says: —

"Yes, I would, Nantaquaus!"

And she laughs and cries, and hugs him close; and Sir Thomas Dale comes and laughs too. All is peace now, he says.

"Since we English and the red beauties will get to marrying," so saith Sir Thomas, "there need be no more war, but blessed peace. Know you what is writ in this letter, my Lady Princess? I see thou dost, by thy roses. Master Rolfe would marry thee — hath doubtless read thee this *billet-doux*."

Thereat Pokahontas hangs down her head and her bosom heaveth.

"But his Majesty King James! What will his Majesty say? Master Rolfe is but a private gentleman, and he would wed a princess. That were *lesé majesté*, I much fear, and his Majesty will grow irate.* But

---

* It is known that his Majesty King James I. *did* "grow irate."

natheless thou shalt marry, poor young people! I will not say thee nay."

Thereat Master Rolfe clasps his hand and cries : —

"Thou art my best friend, Sir Thomas!"

He pumps with Sir Thomas his arm, but the Marshal sudden looks grave, — though I see a wicked smile under it.

"There be but one only hindrance, but that is mighty, Master Rolfe."

"What be that hindrance, Sir Thomas?" saith Master Rolfe quaking.

"The Scripture forbiddeth marrying strange wives ; remember the displeasure the Almighty conceived against the sons of Levi and Israel!"

Thereat Rolfe looks confused and stammers : —

"Natheless"—

"Whereof thy dreams did warn thee, good Master Rolfe!" continues Sir Thomas laughing sudden. "Remember thy perturbations and the troubles of thy distracted soul! Hath the trouble clean gone now?"

I, Anas Todkill, hearing these words, could have gladly caught the Marshal to my breast and cried, "Thanks!" But the laughter endeth, for Master Rolfe would, it seemeth, sink in the ground; and Sir Thomas saith : —

"I did but jest. Why should not you and the Lady Pokahontas marry? Yea, you shall, and a brave wedding."

He turns to my Lady then and says with the bow of a courtier : —

"I will not give you for the men and old muskets now, my little Lady!"

This endeth the talk with them, and Sir Thomas goes apart with Opechancanough (sith the Emperor Powhatan is afraid to come to the English, or will not), and they make terms of peace. The men and pieces shall be brought now and given unto the English; and Sir Thomas will not fulfill his intent to destroy the heathen. Rather he will be close friends with them, since now one of his gentlemen will wed with their princess.

Thus all is soon agreed, and for proof of friendship the ship is loaded with corn; and in two hours the prisoned English are brought and the pieces with 'em. Then my lady puts her arms round Nantaquaus, blushing much the while, and whispers something in his ear, which I know afterwards is this : —

"Thou shalt tell the Emperor, brother

Nantaquaus, and say his wanton would *And so to Jamestown.* have him willing she should marry this English werowance. Thou wilt come to the church; it will be fair with flowers; and tell my sisters Cleopatre and Mata-channa to come too, for maids to the bride, — who will be I."

Thereat she laughs and cries, kissing him, and goes on the ship; and Sir Thomas, firing culverins to show the peace made, sails down York River and so comes again to Jamestown.

Now not to tarry longer here, see how this angel made peace between the English and her own people. She that had saved us now saved them in their time of need. For Sir Thomas had surely ground them between the upper and the nether mill-stone, but for the knowledge that Master Rolfe would wed her and they all would live at peace.

So this angel (God forgive thee, Anas!) was once more the guardian angel of the white and red people in this land of Virginia.*

---

* Todkill's relation of these incidents exactly agrees with that of Raphe Hamor in his *True Discourse of Virginia.* This rare pamphlet also contains Rolfe's letter, a most curious production, and a letter written to London by Sir Thomas Dale precisely corroborating Todkill's narrative.

XIX.

How my Lady Pokahontas asketh, — Must she?

NOW my little Lady would no longer speak to me; nor cared I to speak to her. Sith she hath forgot (I say) him who loved her so dearly, and taken up with this new gallant, even let her go, and the Divell go with her (God forgive thee, Anas!).

But I was wroth, and a man when wroth will foul his lips and his mind, that is worse, with these abominations. Try as I would, I could not forego the memory how *they* walked together in the old days and how she looked at him. Ever she would pluck the wild wood flowers for her hair, and put them therein, and then take them forth and hold 'em out to *him*, and say in her little lisping tongue, "For thee that art the flower of gentilesse and honour!" And now these same flowers were for another love; and this other were the bright, blooming exemplar! Brief, she who had

forgot the man I loved so should be forgot
by me. So I would not go nigh nor speak
to her.

Did she care for that? I knew not,
but many things distracted her thoughts
and time at this season. Sir Thomas Dale,
the valiant and religious High Marshal,
was ever with her. For this soldier was a
man of great knowledge in divinity and
of a good conscience; and would still in-
struct my Lady Pokahontas in the knowledge of our Blessed Saviour.

Now the time comes for her baptism,
and good Master Whitaker performeth it,
sprinkling water on her from the fount in
the church, where attendeth a great multitude. She is new named Rebecca; for
what saith Holy Writ, "And the Lord said
unto her, Two nations are in thy womb,
and two manner of people shall be sepa-
rated from thy bowels;" and further de-
clareth the holy record, Rebekah did con-
ceive twins "and the first came out *red.*"
So she that was to marry an Englishman,
being herself one of a strange people, was
to be called Rebecca, since she would be
mother of two nations.

This done, my Lady and her maidens go
to their vain work of making clothes, and

what not, for the day when she would wed. Oft I go by the window and see 'em sitting within and gabbling, now this, now that; would this ruffle look best, or this ribband, what think you? Jibber-jabber, click-clack! — never was such clatter of tongues! For these farthingales must talk; else for want of it they die (I think). And they talk so they deafen me, and I go by quick not to hear 'em. Not my Lady; she talks but little, and seemeth to care nought for all the finery. Her face is sorrowful, and oft she sitteth with her needle in her hand, looking far away, as one that listens to other things than click-clack. But I go not near her and she cometh not near me, seeming to shun me as I would her.

So passeth the April days, and the flowers are blooming now, and I think, she will have some to deck the church the day she marrieth. 'T will be, sure, a merry wedding! All look to it as a joyous festival wherein two hearts will be joined together in holy matrimony, and so be one, — till they get to scratching! One only seemeth not to look forward thus, a certain sour Anas Todkill. Now and again when he meeteth Master Rolfe he can do no less than scowl at him; and when this same

Master Rolfe goeth to visit the Lady Po- *I take my Lady for a ghost.* kahontas, and I see her blush and look at him softly (through the window which they had best shut), I go off growling.

So as the day is near I take a fancy, I know not how, and one day set out and come to the Place of Retreat on Ware Ridge, where I went with my Captain that day. It is near evening when I get there through the spring woods, and I go up the steep path near overgrown with laurel bushes till I reach the ruinous Fort, whereon the slant sun is now shining. Why I come hither, I say, I know not; for want of other to do, it may be, and to see if I cannot once more catch sight here of him who is here no longer now, being a dead man.

Instead of Smith I see one other, my Lady Pokahontas. She is seated on the very brown stone where she sat by Smith, and crying.

I stop in the edge of the laurel thicket, thinking I see a spirit. Sure the Lady Pokahontas is yonder at Jamestown, in the midst of the click-clack (I say with a shuddering voice), and this is her ghost. But the ghost looks up at the sound of crackling twigs and would fly, but sudden stops.

"Oh, Anas! Is it thou?" she cries. "What brought thee hither?"

With which she covers her face with both hands and begins to weep. I look at her for a time, feeling a great war in my thoughts; but she continueth to sob, and that sound smites me with a great pity, and compassion, and love, so that I haste to her and draw away her hands.

"Let me! let me!" she faltereth. "It is for him that is dead! He was here, thou dost remember. Would I too were dead!"

Could I scoff? Anas Todkill had nevermore thought well of himself had he done so.

"Quiet thee," I say low; "I remember well, and thou too dost remember!"

"Can I forget him?" she says. And then bursts forth all about him, and how she loved him more than all the world; and last, would not marry Master Rolfe, no she would never!

Then cometh a hard thing for Anas Todkill to do. Was I to commend her for this, or say, No, thou must not break faith? Sure this were a vile sin now to counsel this poor maid to show faith by unfaith; and, remaining faithful to the dead, be

faithless by breaking faith with the living. *She will not, and yet she will.*
This comes in my mind, and I say, Steady
Anas! Then to her :—

"Thou must marry Master Rolfe," I say,
with a throb at the heart.

Thereat she looketh at me quick and
saith :—

"I will not! Must I? No, never! How
could I? And yet — yea, I should break
faith."

"Thou must keep thy faith," I say,
"whatever betide; it is I that counsel
thee."

"Dost thou?" she says weeping; "must
I?"

"Yes, thou must."

"Why look at me as thou hast looked of
late, then?" (There was a shot for thee,
Anas!) "But now thou art my truest
friend. See, I listen; must I?"

"We will talk of that," I say as we go
back. "How didst thou come hither?"

I take my Lady's hand and draw her from
the place, for the sun is now near setting;
she telling me 't is but a little way for a
wildwood maid like herself, and she stole
off and came alone.

So we go back through the sunset and
the night to Jamestown, whereof we see

My promise. the lights shining now through the woods and on the water.

"Must I?" she says a last time, stopping ere she reach the Fort.

"Yes," I say.

"And thou — wilt thou still speak to me, and love me, and live with me, nay in my very house? Promise, Anas! then I will obey thee."

She holds my hand and looks in my face, smiling through tears, and I bend down and kiss the little brown hand.

"I will live with thee and be thy henchman till I die," I say. "It is little to promise thee, since twice I owed my life to thee." So then we pass by the Fort and cry, "Friends!" to the guard that challengeth, and my Lady is home.

XX.

My Lady leaneth on a Tree and weepeth.

NOW the wedding of Master Rolfe and *The wedding.* the Lady Pokahontas is over quick. It takes place in the church at Jamestown two days after this talk in the woods of Ware.

Never saw I gayer sight. The cedar pews were wreathed with flowers, for this Virginia land hath divers in April, — what we call the old field daisy and other. Sure the flowers were sweet and heartsome, though I approve not this vain popish fashion of decking the sanctuary with such ; and a great crowd filled the church, (whereof the bells in the west tower were ringing), pushing into the cedar pews quite up to the chancel and walnut communion table. I well remember me the strange sight of buff jerkins and gold-laced doublets rubbing dusky, naked shoulders of Indian chiefs, with feathers on heads, bow in hand. Many heathen had come to see their Lady Pokahontas wed the white face ;

Opachisco makes all laugh.

and the bride marches up the aisle with Master Rolfe and her old uncle Opachisco, a conjurer with a wondrous wrinkled face, and behind these advanceth, with his head up like a young deer of the forest, the lady's best beloved brother Nantaquaus.

My Lady Pokahontas weareth a white robe with down thereon, and a long white veil falling on her shoulders. Her face of a light brown, most like a Spanish maiden's, was all tears and blushes ; and for all the gay scene there was a hid sorrow in her eyes. So Master Rolfe, with some show of bravery in his grave apparel, takes his place on her right hand ; and you may see from his face that all his passion of doubt hath left him ! that he thinketh no more of the sin of marrying strange wives ; but is blithe and glad now. He was near laughing, I think, for joy ; and sudden a great loud laugh greeteth what happens in the church.

Good Master Whitaker, of the Rock Hall parish at Varina, performeth the cere- mony, in his surplice and bands, with rev- erent face above ; and when he says Who giveth this woman ? sudden wrinkled old Opachisco shoves the bride forward so she near falls on the chancel, and says somewhat in his outlandish tongue ; whereat all burst out laughing.

So the two are man and wife, and Nantaquaus comes up and puts both his arms round my Lady and she around him, and they mouth and babble, and I see more tears in her eyes. Then the bells ring once more, and the people talk and shake hands and go about their business.

Of that day I recall no more, being in no good humour, and soon home, till evening when something happens.

I go out in a boat on the James River as though to fish, but in sooth to be by myself and think of this wondrous business. I stay there till nigh sunset, when I paddle in, and coming round a bend of trees, sudden I see my Lady, leaning against that tree Smith leaned on that day when I saw them together.

She is lying against it and weeping, with her robe over her face. She seeth me not and I would not have her; so I come ashore and tie my boat and go back soft to the palisade, thinking my thoughts.

XXI.

Of the City of Henricus and my Lady's Little
Divell that was made a Christian.

NOW see how this strange business cometh to an end at last. She who marries one is yet in love with another, who is dead, *or thought to be,* which were the same. Women (and men too) will still do that, and sure I think Master Will Shakespeare might have writ a drama on this theme. He writ his " Tempest " instead, which is sure a wondrous picture ; but this were greater. For (once more) she that thus marrieth one, loveth another with all her heart ; only she consoleth herself by saying low, " My true love is dead."

Natheless fate is strong and the years be hard masters. He that is dead, though he be not forgot, is no longer here ; so my Lady goeth weeping to her bridal and is now Mistress Rolfe.

I say not she continueth to weep. She is young yet ; and that blessed youth is like the sap of a tree which will push strong to cover up a gash in the trunk, be it never so deep. My Lady gets back her smiles now, and ere long she findeth somewhat more to think of than dead loves, in two little black eyes that stare at her, while a red mouth babbles.

This not at Jamestown, but at Master Rolfe his plantation, called Farmingdell, not far from the City of Henricus, on the upper waters of the James River. Now a word, ere I pass to other matters, of this famous city of Henricus at Varina, — so named after his Highness the noble Prince Henry, who ere long dieth, — whereof the founder was Sir Thomas Dale, the High Marshal of Virginia. Though this true relation of my Lady Pokahontas be writ for that great dame's honour, and most I would speak of her, yet somewhat too of things in the first Virginia days ; which in years to come may be read by Virginia people with some little interest (perchance).

For when my Lord la Ware sends out his Lieutenant Governor, Sir Thomas Gates, in the year 1611, the High Marshal his hands are free, and with some three hundred men he goes up James River and founds this City of Henricus at Varina. Arrohattox is the name of the country

Hope-in-Faith there.

there, being one of the five domains which descended to the Emperor Powhatan from his ancestors; and never saw you so strange a sight as the river is there. It runneth this way and that, most like a great snake wriggling as he dieth; and where the city was built is in a peninsula, where the river maketh a great loop; so that, after some seven miles, it cometh back to one hundred yards of the same place. This narrow neck is a defence against Indians, and is called the "Dutch Gap," — for by order of Sir Thomas his Dutch people begin to dig a channel there to let the river through, but stop the work.

Now the city is soon built on the plateau inside, with three streets, a fair church, and a palisade across the narrow neck; also one two miles long from river to river outside in the main.* On the south bank is another palisade, which incloseth a great tract, and Forts Charity and Patience, Hope-in-Faith and Mount Milado; also Rock Hall, Master Whitaker's parsonage. And now if you ask me why *Hope-in-Faith*, which be a Puritan name, I answer 't was I that named it, and Sir Thomas Dale saith : —

* The main land.

"Content! Thou shalt call it such, Mas- I am to be welcome.
ter Anas! Thou wert once a conspira-
tor and nigh I would bore thy tongue,
but thou art a true man now, Heaven be
thanked."

But to tell of my Lady, and how I came
to live with her here. Whenas Master
Rolfe would go from Jamestown to this
plantation called Farmingdell, near Henricus, he saith to me, looking grave and
friendly : —

"Hast thou not promised some one
something, Master Todkill ? "

"Doubtless men promise many things,
Master Rolfe," I say, making show I un-
derstand not.

"What thou hast promised, good Anas,
is to live with my Lady," he says; "and
now as a worthy man thou must keep it.
If thou come to my home thou shalt be
welcome as my Lady's old and true friend,
and perchance thou might write somewhat
for me, since Sir Thomas would have me
for Secretary of the Colony."

This pleases me much; but I would not
say yes, all of a sudden, lest my grum looks
at this happy couple (thinking of Smith)
make me unwelcome. But a voice comes
behind me while I ponder so : —

I go to Farming-dell.

"Thou didst promise me!"

And I turn quick and see my Lady, one foot lifted and her face wet as she looks at me.

"Thou didst say thou wouldst!" she murmurs.

And there that ends. I go to Farming-dell, and am made much of there, and have a good room which my Lady would still tend with her own hands, making all things neat when the maid had gone. The house is a good house, with a palisade against Indians, and Master Rolfe hath rich low grounds where he showeth me he can raise the wild weed tobacco; for he hath done so.* I talk with him thereon and cry:—

"Fie! wouldst thou? Why plant this foul weed that leadeth only to imbecility?" But he laughs and says, It is a comfort to man, and not forbid by Holy Writ; he himself hath come to love it, and smokes his pipe while he thinks.

Now to speak no more of tobacco, whereof his Majesty King James hath just writ his "Counterblast," somewhat happens

---

* This accords with the statement in Hamor's *True Discourse*, that Rolfe first domesticated this plant, hitherto wild, in the year 1612, which was just before Todkill's coming. "Farmingdell" was just below Varina; and the region was so called by Sir Thomas Dale from the fact that the tobacco raised there was so fine as to resemble the sweet-scented Spanish *Verinas* of the West Indies.

at this house of Farmingdell which happeneth oft elsewhere. My Lady keepeth
her chamber a little while, and then cometh
forth with a young Master Rolfe, whom she
holdeth up to me, and saith with bright
eyes : —

"Saw you ever such a wanton, Anas !"

Thereat she putteth the boy in my arms
and saith to him : —

"Go to thy best friend, child, who is the
best friend of thy mother ! "

And the child hugs to me and lays his
face against my beard and is content there ;
whereupon I begin to love him, and love
him more and more as the days pass.

I would have him named John Smith —
this Smith being (so to say) a friend of
the family in old years ; but I say not this
to any one, much more to my Lady, for fear
her tears come. And they say he shall be
named Thomas.*

The christening of Master Thomas Rolfe
was a great merrymaking at Varina, and

---

* The birthplace of Thomas Rolfe, the only child of Pokahontas,
has heretofore been a disputed question. The only record elsewhere
is in the *General History*, where it is said: " *During this time* the
Lady Rebecca, *alias* Pokahontas, daughter to Powhatan, by the dili-
gent care of Master Iohn Rolfe, her husband, and his friends, was well
instructed in Christianity; she had also by him a child, which she
loved most dearly." Thomas Rolfe was thus a Virginian by birth,
and persons of note descended from him, — among others, John
Randolph of Roanoke.

hugely delighted Sir Thomas, who had his home there, as also Master Whitaker, as the first-fruits of heathennesse, and the promise of the New Jerusalem. For this Marshal Dale was a student of divinity, which be rare, as I said, in a martial man. He and good Master Whitaker, parson of Rock Hall parish, who is called in England the "Apostle of Virginia," are close friends, as is fit. For this Master Whitaker is a true man, who hath left his warm nest at home to come to the new land; where soon he writes his "Good News from Virginia," wherein he crieth, "Awake, you true Englishmen! remember the Plantation is God's and the reward your country's!" *

Sorrowful am I to say that ere two twelvemonths have passed, this good Apostle of Virginia, who saith he will stay "till he be called hence," is called hence by God; he being drowned by the upsetting of his boat, in crossing the James River from Rock Hall to Henricus.

As yet he laboureth and catechiseth the children, Indian and others, in the new school of Henricus; certain axe-men and men-at-arms, too, that would hear the

---

* This pamphlet, containing an earnest appeal for help to convert the Indians, was published in the very year Todkill's relation has now reached — 1613.

blessed message. He is ever at Sir Thomas *He christens the child.* Dale his house, and they dispute on divinity; but sudden all stops when Pokahontas her child is to be christened.

It is done in Varina church, and Master Whitaker, who hath married my Lady, now takes in his arms her child, and sprinkleth water on him, whereat he laughs and babbles; and then we go out, while my Lady holds him, and kisses him, looking at him with mother's eyes that would eat him; for in sooth she loveth him dearly. So back to the Farmingdell house, and my Lady looks happy and content; and I must fain hold the boy, and say to him, as he nestleth to me:—

" Thou little Divell that art now a Christian! I wish thee well!"

Now my Lady stayeth but this time (yet) in Virginia, and I continue her henchman; and we talk together much, oft of him who is gone. At such time she looketh at me with sad eyes, and then to her husband, as though to say, "Do not thou think ill of me if I love still a dead one I once loved." Sure never was more gracious creature than this Lady Pokahontas; and to be beside her was my chiefest happiness. But to write more hereof would weary; and with somewhat more (not much) of what takes place in this land of Virginia, we will go back home to England.

But first of what maketh me laugh much, how I see again the Emperor Powhatan and on what business we went. Since her wedding Master Rolfe, he and my Lady see each the other no more — why, I know not. He would have it so, and sendeth her word (they say) she must now live with him she weddeth, and not come back to the woods : if he ever visiteth the English (which he will not), he will be to see her.

But they have commerce and good will,* and to and fro cometh the Emperor's henchman, a deformed humpback they call Rawhunt, bringing venison and what not, with the King's love to his child. She sendeth back what will please him, as beads and such stuff ; and writeth something on willow bark in strange figures, what I know not.

Scarce I think to see the great Emperor more, but that time now cometh, whereof I will speak. But first, this Rawhunt is *Caliban* in Master Shakespeare his " Tempest,"

---

* This is also the statement of the old historian Stith, writing in the next century.

as I after know. From the first he hath *Who was Miranda.*
come to Jamestown, to and back, and they
that go to England report of him, as of
Pokahontas. Whereof cometh knowledge to Master Shakespeare, who
useth all; making his strange
Caliban of this dwarf, as
his *Miranda* of my
Lady Pokahon-
tas.

XXII.

Of the Trick the High Marshal would play on the Emperor, but he would not.

I see the Emperor for the last time.

BUT to speak, ere we go from Virginia, of my last look at the great Powhatan. Sure never was such food for laughter as on this visit to the Emperor. Even now, long after, when I think of it I burst out sudden, so that they around me cry, "What aileth thee?" and I answer, "I but bethink me of old days in the woods of Virginia, with his highness the Emperor Powhatan."

It comes about in this wise. I have told ofttimes what manner of man was the builder of Henricus city, the mighty and valiant Sir Thomas Dale, who, though none exceeded him in divinity as in courage, was a subtle master of policy and would gain good ends by crooked ways; whereof this showeth.

Though the Indians were now peaceful, yet they never were safe; and the bruit coming to our ears that the Paspaheghs *We find him at Machot.* and Nansemunges were ill affected toward us, Sir Thomas Dale bethinks him to make sure of them by this strange device: (namely) Powhatan was their Emperor, and to have from him a hostage, which Master Raphe Hamor was sent to get. This was Powhatan's young daughter Cleopatre, sister of my Lady Pokahontas, whereof you shall see by this relation, and what honour the High Marshal designed her.

I, Anas Todkill, was one of the party sent to visit King Powhatan; and going by the desert* we came to Machot, where we found the King in his great arbour, with a guard of two hundred bowmen. He was seated on his couch of mats with his wives and chiefs about him, and offered us a pipe of tobacco; whereafter he would know our errand. Master Hamor then riseth and saith : —

"I come from your Brother Dale, and would speak with you in private."

At this the King studied a little, and sent out all but his two queens that always did sit by him, and the interpreter,

---

* In the old relations this word is used in the sense of *thicket* or *wilderness*: as the "desert of Pamunkey," meaning the thick woods wholly uninhabited. Machot was at the present West Point on the York.

who was that same young Henry Spilman, my cousin, saved from death by dear Pokahontas.

"Now speak," says the King (or Emperor), "for I listen."

As he said these words, he stretched his legs out of his raccoon-skin robe and kicked a brand on to the fire so awkward that all laughed, but he looked grave.

Then Master Hamor, looking at him, says : —

"Your Brother Dale sends you this copper and these blue beads, also these two knives, and will send you also a grindstone if you listen to what he asks."

"What does Brother Dale ask?" the King says by his interpreter, viewing the beads and the rest ; whereat Master Hamor clears his throat and thus answers : —

"The bruit of the exquisite perfection of your youngest daughter, being spread through all your territories, hath come to the hearing of your Brother Dale, who hath sent me. He entreats you as his brother to permit this maiden to return with me."

"Return !" cries the King suddenly ; "why return ?"

"For her sister's desire to see her ; and another end still."

"What end?" says his Majesty; "why *He would wed the Emperor's daughter.* desireth Brother Dale to see my child?"

"He would gladly make her his nearest companion, wife, and bedfellow."

But the King would hardly hear Master Hamor. He moves about and gets up; now and then he kicks brands on the fire; once he pulls his wife's ears, and then sits down, muttering. But Master Hamor would not notice these signs that his errand was not to the King's desire.

"Hear me to an end," he says to Powhatan: whereat the Emperor leaneth back as though asleep.

"The reason whereof your Brother Dale would make your daughter his wife is to rivet a natural union between us, and ever be friends. He himself means to dwell in Virginia while he liveth, and would have perpetual friendship."

Then hearing that this is the end, the King rises and kicks at the fire, and then speaks thus by his interpreter: —

"I gladly accept Brother Dale's salute, but my daughter whom he desireth I sold within these few days past, to be wife to a great werowance, for two bushels of roanoke (which is their money), and she is gone three days' journey from me."

But Master Hamor would not hearken, and said : —

" Your greatness and power is such that, to gratify Brother Dale, you might give up the roanoke and take back your daughter from that chief. She is not yet twelve years old, and should yet tarry a space. This meaneth your Brother Dale, who entreats you to spare her."

But the Emperor shakes his head, forgetting his vain story of the great werowance (his daughter being there with him).

"I love my child dear as my own life," he says, "and though I have many children, I delight in none so much as her. If I did not often behold her I could not possibly live; and if she lived with you at your Fort, you know I could not see her. You have one daughter now; when she dieth you shall have another; but she yet liveth. So no more ; and now to tell me of my daughter Pokahontas and my unknown son. How do they like, live, and love together?"

Master Hamor, in no gay mood at being disappointed, says : —

" Your daughter is so well content that she would not change her life to return

and live with you again, though you be-
sought her."

Thereat Powhatan laughs heartily, and says: "I am very glad of it:" and again lies down on his bed, now and then laughing a little at his thoughts. Soon he sits up once more, as who should say, Art thou done now? and will not hearken any more, but trifles the time, playing with his blue beads. Last he sends his Brother Dale this greeting: None of his people shall trouble us; and adds, proudly: "I, which have power to perform it, have said it."

So homeward, and ere long we are back at the city of Henricus, where my Lady Pokahontas listens to our adventure and sighs, and I think her old wood life cometh back to her. At what Master Hamor reporteth, Sir Thomas Dale says, laughing:

"So be it; I am content, and perchance 't is better. I scarce could make up this matter of the new wife with my Lady Dale! The white cat in London would certes scratch the Virginia kitten."

And so that trick of the High Marshal comes to this conclusion.*

---

* Todkill's account of this singular embassy is identical with Hamor's in the work before mentioned, *A True Discourse of the Estate of Virginia.* Lady Dale, wife of Sir Thomas, is there mentioned as then living.

XXIII.

My Lady goes to England.

NOW this year, 1616, Sir Thomas Dale, our valiant Governor, would go back to England and take my Lady Pokahontas with him, to show the first-fruits of God's mercy in converting these poor heathen to the knowledge of our blessed Saviour.

My Lady goes willingly, and Master Rolfe and her boy with her, whereto Powhatan joins one of his people, called Uttamatomakkin, to count the English with a notched stick (which he throws away after a little while). And, further, this savage was to know if Captain Smith were dead; whereof a strange bruit comes to us, and so to him, that his old friend still liveth. But they would not tell my Lady Pokahontas.

So toward early spring of the said year (1616) we embark for England, for I would go back with my Lady; and soon we drop down the great river, and so out of the capes into the wide ocean. Certes I was sorrowful at this going away from the Vir- *We come to Plymouth.* gin land, and stood quiet nigh the helm, looking where the sun was setting, and thinking my thoughts of the old days and God's good providence, above all in sending succour in that woful Starving Time.

"He that shall but turn up his eye," I say, standing on the ship, "and behold but the spangled canopy of heaven above him, must needs see God's mercy, and how He inclineth all things to the help of them that trust in Him."

Thus saying in a low voice full of thanks and praise, as I stood in the dusk light on the ship, I was ware of some one weeping, and turned and saw my Lady not far from me. She sits looking back to Virginia, her face lying in her hand, and her body shaking. Whereat, thinking not to disturb her, I go away softly, leaving her to her thoughts.

Now with favouring winds we come to Plymouth in England, and the bruit goes abroad that the princess Pokahontas is on board the ship, and Sir Thomas Stukely, the Company's man, comes and bows low to her.* Then a lord arrives post haste from London, bearing a message from his

---

* This person afterwards took charge of Pokahontas' son.

Majesty, who would see my Lady Pokahontas, and receive her near him as a royal princess, with due honour to the blood royal (though she be a savage).

So we go to London, and take lodging at Brentford, nigh the great city and the palace of Kew, whereto resort many of the fine gentlemen and ladies to visit my princess become a great personage. The King would have her with him, and meets her with gracious words, giving orders she shall be well placed at the masques, and attended royally. Thither she went, and to the Globe Theatre too (whereof more anon), and was much liked of her Majesty the Queen, who kisses her on both cheeks and calls her "my child," smiling graciously. Master Rolfe goes with her, but is not received with such honours: no, not so much as with the least favour, most of all by his Majesty the King.

At the first reception of my Lady, her husband goes with her, and his Majesty comes and raises her when she would kneel, looking at her kindly. But when Master Rolfe bends knee too before him, his royal face grows of a sudden very black. The King knits together his eyebrows and says, grunting out his anger: —

"Would you! would you! Who would *Master Rolfe* have you, for a false loon, marry a princess, *his disfavour.* when nothing but my subject, and never say even 'By your leave'!"

Whereat he sudden turns his back on him, puffing and showing him other discourtesy; and Master Rolfe, much abashed, goes back to the crowd and is no more seen that day.[*]

Never saw I such honour paid any mortal as my little Lady. Sudden she grows the fashion, and my Lord Bishop of London gives a great entertainment at his palace of Lambeth to her honour; whereof Master Pepys is heard to say 't is the finest he has ever seen there. Ever to Brentford come fine coaches by day and night, with earls and ladies, footmen and outriders, and flambeaux carried in front, to visit my Lady. They all go away praising her, and saying they have seen many English ladies worse favoured, proportioned, and behavioured.

"Pardie," I hear my Lord la Ware say to his honourable Lady, as they get back to their coach, "She is a wonder, this young princess, and 't is easy to see her

---

[*] This displeasure of James I., which is given by Stith, the old historian, as a " constant tradition " in Virginia, is thus verified by Todkill.

Smith is not dead. blood be royal. She carrieth herself as the daughter of a King!" *

My Lady takes all quietly, with much content and satisfaction, but ever I see on her face what brings back to me the memory of the month of August in her Virginia, when the fields are bright at one moment, but sudden a cloud shadow floats over, and they are darkened. The bruit comes Smith is not dead, and I remember when she first set eyes on him, though she (then) had no speech with him; whereof this further relation will show the time and place.

One day comes a message from the Queen's Majesty; there will be a Virginia play at the Globe Theatre: Master Shakespeare's "Tempest," whereof the stage is the Bermudas islands, now by charter † a part of Virginia. Her Majesty is going, and indeed has commanded the play, and would have my Lady Pokahontas be present too.

"Content: say to the Queen I will attend her," says my little Lady with her royal air (she speaks good English now for a long time). So the lord that brings

* This seems to have been the general comment at the time on the bearing of Pokahontas.
† The new charter of 1612.

the message bows low, and goes away; *My Lady's anguisb.*
and my Lady says, " You must go too,
Anas."

" What! I, a good Puritan, seek a play-
house! That were a sin," I say laughing;
but my Lady will not smile. She looks so
sorrowful that my heart bleeds, and says
lowly : —

" I would go away, if only in my heart,
from this London, and be in Virginia, if
but for a poor hour, and forget myself."

She stops and muses, with her eyes
moist, and a sudden blush.

" They say he is not dead! " she whispers.

" Not dead ? Who has told you that ? "
I cry, knowing she meaneth Smith.

" I have but now learned the truth," she
says, speaking with a great sob and covering her face. " O me! why am I not dead
—sith he lives ! "

Whereat she bendeth down and crieth,
and I (lest I do likewise) go out hastily.

11

XXIV.

I go to the Globe Theatre.

The Play-house. TOWARD evening, nigh sunset, comes a coach sent by the Queen's Majesty, with four horses and flambeau-bearers, to take my Lady to the play. None is in the big coach, whereof the laced footman bows low as he bangs to the door, but my Lady Pokahontas and Master Rolfe, with myself, Anas Todkill.

Sure this was tempting Providence, to venture into that abode of sin called a play-house, which the Puritan hateth ; but then this " Tempest " of Master Shake-speare were doubtless a goodly spectacle ! and if I, Anas Todkill, grow ever to be a preacher warning the brethren against sin, certes, knowledge of the Devil's wiles and how he ensnareth souls would be to the purpose. So (in short) I went to the Globe.

The play-house was even then filled, my Lady's coming being no doubt known ; and in the rooms around the gallery in front, over which was a thatched roof, sat many noble lords and ladies in grand dresses, with jewels on them, among the rest my Lord Southampton, the friend and patron of Master Shakespeare. Below these, in the open space which is uncovered, stood the common sort, drinking beer and smoking tobacco pipes, and ever taking these from their mouths to look up to the gentry and talk of them.

The stage in front had two curtains opening in the middle, and through that opening was seen the tapestry and the raised balcony behind, with two private rooms on either hand for great people attending the play. One of these was fitted up royally for her Majesty, who would attend on this evening : and my Lady Pokahontas with Master Rolfe and myself were shown to it.

Now the night was near come, and the flambeaux were lighted around, and at last a great stamping and shouting says the Queen is here. She enters with her attendants (but not his Majesty) ; and, kissing my Lady on both sides her face, bids the players come in and begin.

Many, doubtless, that read this relation have seen acted this great play of the

The Tempest. "Tempest." A decade before, the worthy reader will remember, Smith talked with Master Shakespeare thereof at the *Mermaid* Tavern; and now the play was writ. That talk of the Isles of Devils put the Bermudas in Master Shakespeare's head,* and from Master Strachey's book, the "Wrack and Redemption of Sir Thomas Gates," he gets his story. See how the English fleet (save the *Sea-Venture*) gets safe to the Chesapeake Bay; and Shakespeare's fleet (save the King's ship) to the Mediterranean flote. Master Strachey tells of the strange light that burned on the masts and yards of the *Sea-Venture;* and tricksy *Ariel,* saith he, *flamed amazement on the topmast, the yards and bowsprit; and hid the King's ship in the still vex'd Bermoothes,* which the Spaniard calleth our *Bermudas.*†

Sure never was greater writer than this Master Will Shakespeare, who passeth quick from that terrible *Lear* and the woes of *Hamlet* to the merriest fancies. No sooner stalketh by mournful *Macbeth* than

---

* Todkill here forgets that before the meeting at the *Mermaid* Shakespeare had already been impressed by the "still vex'd Bermoothes" as a fit stage for a weird drama.

† Todkill here verifies an interesting fact — that the wreck of the *Sea-Venture* suggested the *Tempest.*

Touchstone comes laughing : and that mad knight Sir *John Falstaff* waddles close on gibing *Richard.* Oft I wept, or shouted with laughter, seeing these — but what write I ? There cometh the cat forth of a sudden from the bag. Anas Todkill a frequenter of the play-house ! But be honest (I say), Anas ; and then thou wert away from thy home, in big London, and thy bad exemplar not seen ; when the days to preach of these deadly sins cometh, thou wilt know and denote such truly.*

Sitting in the room beside the balcony, my Lady Pokahontas would listen modestly while her Majesty talked to her, answering quietly, with simple mien, as of a poor maiden, but yet a King's daughter too. The stage was full of gallants, who would sit on stools by the side tapestries, and smoke tobacco pipes, ever laughing. When the boys anon passed, dressed as women (for there be no true women on our stage in England), these same gallants would pluck them by the sleeve, and make as though they would steal kisses ; whereat my Lady would laugh a little, and say she marvelled they were so ill-mannered. But

---

* This reflection, from its repetition, seems to have afforded much comfort to Master Anas Todkill.

Mad-caps.   the maid of honour that sat by her whis-
pered "They were mad-caps, and ever
would do with herself the same, in the very
Queen's palace."

XXV.

And meet again with Captain Smith and Master Shakespeare.

NIGHT had come now a long time, *Nonparella.* and the flambeaux were spouting out smoke, and the crowd below was shouting and moving to and fro, most at *Caliban.*

He had a hump on his back, and would growl and laugh like a dog barking, showing great tushes ; so that the crowd would cry out he was hag-born, a divell — and would *Ariel* the little sprite but play him some trick.

My Lady looks most at *Ariel,* but sudden listens when *Caliban* saith *Prospero* calleth *Miranda* his *Nonpareil.* Thereat she turneth a little white, and her bosom under her ruff rises and falls like two waves, and she catcheth her breath.

Why is this (I say) ; what aileth my Lady ? But quick I know that she thinketh of one who called *her* the Nonpareil of Virginia —

my dear and noble Captain, once her love. He would ever call her such, saying the whole world had not her like; and she laughed one day in Virginia, and said : —

" Then her name was not Matoaka since *he* had called her *Nonparella.*"

And now the name strikes her sudden and woful, as she hears it in the play.

I bend over, and looking close at her say in a low voice : —

" What would you ? I know who hath been with Master Shakespeare, and of whom he hath been talking."

At that her head droops down and she studies the floor for a little while, growing quiet as she museth. But a new thing to try my Lady's strength is to come. Across the balcony of the stage was, I said, a second private room, with tapestry in front, facing the Queen's. Up to nigh the end of the play this room was not open, and the tapestry in its front hung down, hiding the inner. Now this was thrust back, and running on a stick made some noise, whereat I look thither, and see in the shadow Master Shakespeare and Captain Smith.

I look sudden to my Lady, and see she is looking too. She is white as her smock, and trembles a little, with her eyes fixed *He sees her too.* on Smith. Sudden she puts her hand on my arm and whispers faint : —

"He is not dead, you see; it was a lie they told! He is not dead! he is not dead!"

"It is he himself and no other" (these words I could only say in a voice well nigh stifled); "and look! he sees you. Certes he comes to-night to see two Nonparellas at the play."

Smith was nigh lost in the shadow of the tapestry, but I could see his face. He was no older to my eyes, for men like this are always young, methinks. The broad forehead showed some care, but the eyes were clear, and the long mustachios that he ever wore could not hide the frank mouth whereon was writ his nature. He was looking at my Lady Pokahontas with a long, still gaze, and then I knew he had heard she was coming, and had come himself to see her. Sudden I rose up.

"You would go see him?" my Lady says in a whisper.

"Certes; my heart beats at very sight of him."

"And mine," she says shaking. "Tell him — no, tell him nothing!"

I go quick to him.

And with a great sob she turns away and leans back in shadow.

I go out and meet a play-man, who tells me how I may come to the room where Smith is. I near stumbled down a trap wherefrom rises the ghost of *Hamlet* and such other unearthly shapes, and got to the room and went in. Smith was leaning to one side in the shadow of the curtain, but Master Shakespeare sate erect, smiling courteously as friends saluted him from the theatre below.

I touched Smith on the shoulder, and turning round he says, low : —

" Is it thou, Anas ? "

" Your old soldier and henchman ; yes, I say."

" None was ever truer," he says, in a strange, altered voice. " I saw you yonder, and my Lady Rebecca."

He spoke so coldly that I marvelled, and said : —

" Why call you her the Lady Rebecca ? That is her name with the court people, but certes with you she is the blessed Pokahontas."

Thereat he colours up and groans.

" It is the same," he says, "since I am now naught to her. But no more of that,

Anas, — or here at least; this is no place for speech.   I came hither to-night to see her, having no strength to meet her and talk with her; but I have writ the Queen of her great merit and how she saved us."

"Not meet and talk with her!" I say; "not with her, thy saviour?"

"My undoer!" he saith groaning. "But this hubbub killeth speech.   I know you lodge at Brentford, which is not so far, and, if you please, we will walk thither after the play.   Shall we?"

"Yes, indeed."

"I will tell you my mind, then.   I am going away soon, and come but in time to get a last look of my Lady the Princess.   I lodge at the *Mermaid*, and my friend Master Shakespeare, coming to London, meets me there.   This in front of us is he; sure you remember him, since you once talked with him."

The noise of the theatre was such as kept Master Shakespeare from hearing us. Now his name being spoken behind him he turns round quick and I am face to face with him.

He is clad in a slashed doublet with plain ruff, and shows some bravery: but 't was not this man's clothes that people

Whereof he talked with me. looked at, but his face.   Never saw I face so friendly, or smile sweeter.   He wears a mustache, and a pointed beard on his chin (we now call a *royale*), and is growing bald ; but that only better shows his wondrous forehead, that piled-up mountain whence he dug *Macbeth* and *Lear*.   Once 't was hard to fancy he had ever a serious thought, or cared for aught save some gay conceit ; but I see now what seemeth a shadow on his face.

" Is it somewhat that hath troubled him (I say) as the time hath gone on ? "

But his old courtesy is unchanged, and his fine-filed phrase, ever as he speaks, is the same.   He knows me quick, though 't is more than a decade since that day at the *Mermaid* tavern, and shakes my hand, calling me by name.

So I had lived all these years in Virginia ? (he saith smiling.)   Would he himself could have left this England, which bustleth so, and ventured under the west wind to that land of lands !   The Fount of Youth was to be found there, people said, which he would fain try, since he groweth old and bald now! (he laugheth and pointeth to his forehead).   Is yonder truly the Princess Pokahontas ? he asks.   His friend Captain Smith hath told him how she *Our talk endeth.* once saved him, and he hath figured her in his *Miranda*, that is, *One to be wondered at;* as see where Miranda cries, " Beseech you, father ! Sir, have pity ; I 'll be his surety !" when *Prospero* would smite down *Ferdinand* as Powhatan would smite Smith. This *Ferdinand* is Smith, he says laughing, though a king's son; and *Caliban* is a deformed Indian, one Rawhunt, whereof Smith hath oft told him ; which *Caliban* saith in the play that *Duke Prospero* calleth *Miranda* his " Nonpareil," which is what Captain Smith calleth the Lady Pokahontas.

With such pleasant talk Master Will Shakespeare leaneth back, smiling; and I scarce believe that this is really he that writ the terrible-mournful " Othello," " Lear," and " Hamlet." He is just the same as other people ; and when Master Heminge, one of the players, comes in to talk with him of printing his plays, he laughs and trifles the time, saying 't is a small matter ; he will think of it. And when Master Heminge urges him, Master Shakespeare crieth with mock earnest : " Away ! life is but a shadow !" and that he hath more important business, which is to go back to Stratford and see how grow certain calves of his !

We say farewell.

So at last the play ends; and Master Shakespeare gets up and says Will we go to the *Mermaid* tavern, where he lodgeth, and empty a cup of sack with him? Fain would I, Anas Todkill, Puritan though I be, go with this writer of plays, had not the meeting with Smith moved me so. He, too, would talk with me, so we tell Master Shakespeare another time, whereof my regret remaineth still.

For 't was the last sight I ever had of that wonder of the time and all times (I think). He was never in London more. On the next day he rides, as I hear, for Stratford, and the same month dies of a fever there. So we lost him that was our delight, and all England, nay the world, holdeth not to-day his like.

XXVI.

*How Smith telleth he was not dead, and crieth,
"O Heaven ! could she not wait ?"*

THE Queen goes from the theatre now, *Back to Brentford.*
and ere long my Lady Pokahontas,
and Master Rolfe too, in their coach to
Brentford. I go not with 'em, making ex-
cuse to my Lady, who looks at me with a
long look. The flambeaux light her face
for but a moment, and then she is gone.

With Smith I walk back to Brentford ;
and to-day, shutting my eyes, I can see
and hear all things on this night, which
was April and a bright moon shining.

We talk long, walking slow, and Smith
tells me all. He went away from Virginia
loving the Lady Pokahontas with his heart
of hearts ("with every drop of blood in
my heart, Anas !" he crieth groaning), and
thinking she loves him ; but now see what
cometh ! When he went he was sore tormented by his hurt on the boat coming
from the Falls, and needeth a chirurgeon ;

but most he went to London to confound his enemies. Then he would come back to Virginia and take Pokahontas for his. But ever (he said) his enemies fretted him, and kept him fighting 'em for his very good name, till he was well nigh in despair. He would not stay longer in London then, and sets out in a ship for Virginia; but off the Azores is made prisoner by a French ship and carried to Rochelle, when he is reported dead and scarce escapes with his life to England.*

Thereat I smite my hands together and cry : —

"This news cometh to Virginia, and the Lady Pokahontas is in despair!"

"Is it so?" he saith, with a grim look. "Nay, this thing hight the heart of a woman scarce hath time to despair, ere some brave new lover cometh!"

"Thou art unjust!" I cry. "When the rumour cometh, it well nigh breaketh her heart!"

"Is it so?" he saith again. "Well, my own near breaks when the bruit comes to

---

* This was possibly the origin of the rumour of Smith's death. He says in the *General History* that going in a boat to Rochelle "the Captain was drowned and half his company the same night: and ere long many of them that escaped drowning told me *the newes they heard of my owne death.*"

me she is married to Rolfe. O Heaven!
could she not wait?"

"She thought thee dead."

"Or he maketh her think it!"

"I wot not. So far as I know he thinketh likewise. All in the colony believe it,
and my Lady hideth herself in despair. She
goes to Potomac, not to live in the midst of
places you and she were together in, and
Argall, that hawk, goes and betrays her;
and when she comes to Jamestown it is
said by all that you are dead."

Thereat he hangs his head, and, musing,
says in a low voice: —

"Is it even so?"

No more; and I add these words: —

"Blame her not, worthy friend and
Captain. Long she mourned for thee,
and would not listen to this Master Rolfe
or any other: of which thou shalt have
proof."

Whereat I tell him all, and of that last
meeting with her at the Place of Retreat.
He listens, silent, with his brows knit piteously and his breast heaving. I see the
moonlight on his face, and hear him groan.

"Be it so," he saith at last; "this is the
end, Anas."

So no more of Pokahontas then, save that

12

He would sail for New England. he hath writ the Queen a letter telling of all her goodness to the Colony and himself, and that he will come to see her ere long, and take his last greeting of her, at Brentford. Soon he will sail for New England, and were content to have it his last voyage; not to Virginia,—he will go there no more.

Having come thus far to Brentford, he leaves me and goes back to London, slow, in the moonlight. I stand looking after him for a long time, till his form is no more seen, and then I go home thinking. What I think to myself is this: "Were I to talk with Master Shakespeare and tell him this history, certes there were matter in it for a greater play than even his fine 'Tempest'!"

XXVII.

Of the Valiant Captain Smith's Last Greeting with my Lady Pokahontas.

NOW to end this true relation of my Smith comes to see my Lady. Lady and her soldier, the next day Smith comes to Brentford with divers courtiers and other his acquaintances, seeking to have it believed 't is only a visit as of any one to this married Princess (no longer his love, but a Christian woman, having nought to do with that now).

He goes not in at first with my Lord Southampton and the rest, — this Southampton being the same whereto Master Shakespeare writes his famed sonnets. Smith draws me apart to the garden, and says he will show me something; then the rest being gone, he will speak a little with my Lady, and bid her farewell. We find a nook, and sit on a bench there, and he draws forth a paper. Therewith he heaves a great sigh and says : —

"How sorrowful is this world, Anas! I thought to wed my little Princess, but 't is vain now, and here is the end. But to show you this."

And he unwraps his paper, writ in his bold hand as though with his good sword's point.

" Hearing the Virginia ship is at Plymouth with my Lady and her husband," he says, " I fell into great amaze and wist not what to do, Anas. But to do duty is always best, and I write this paper to her Majesty ; whereof hear these few words."

So he reads in a low voice, broke with sighs, this short discourse : —

" Most admired Queen, the love I bear my God, my King, and country hath so oft emboldened me in the worst of extreme dangers, that my honesty doth constrain me to present your Majesty this. That some ten years ago, being in Virginia and taken prisoner by Powhatan, their chief King, I received from this great savage exceeding great courtesy, especially from his son Nantaquaus, the most manliest, comeliest, boldest spirit I ever saw in a savage, and his sister Pokahontas, the King's most dear and well-beloved daughter, being but a child of twelve or thirteen years of age, whose compassionate, pitiful heart of my desperate estate gave me much cause to respect her. She hazarded the beating out *His enemies would malign him.* of her own brains to save mine ; and not only that, but so prevailed with her father that I was safely conducted to Jamestown."

Here he stops and says, lowly : —

" Know you, Anas, that my enemies would say this is not true ? So they hate me for being Master yonder that I am perforce a brave liar ! I make up this story, though nought is here to my own honour, save it be to a soldier's honour that a woman is pitiful to him."

" Your enemies say that ? " I cry out. " Why at Jamestown we all know it, and my Lady tells it a thousand times, as do her wild train of people who came to the Fort with her ! "

" That is nought ! I am a Gascon, and boast of what I have done ! " he says, his voice sounding bitter. " Natheless, let the ill tongues wag. She herself is here to speak now, and may say if it be not true."

" Certes, that is the end of it, worthy Captain," I say.

" I know not. The men I lashed from Virginia would destroy my character, Anas. They dare not face me, but will skulk, and write down that which at length, in

He careth not.

the after time, will blacken my memory. Who knoweth? After all my hazards in that great land of America, it may be that my memorial will perish with me, since I 've writ nothing." *

"Never!" I say. "Fear not that, thou brave soldier and true heart."

"Let it be so. I stand on mine own feet, and my life is my answer; now to finish these few words."

And he reads what follows from the paper writ to her Majesty.

"And this relief, most gracious Queen, was commonly brought us by this Lady Pokahontas. Notwithstanding all these passages when inconstant fortune turned our peace to war, this tender virgin would still not spare to dare to visit us, and by her our jars have been oft appeased and our wants still supplied. (Thou knowest whether this be true or not, Anas.) Were it the policy of her father thus to employ her, or the ordinance of God thus to make her his instrument, or her extraordinary affection to our nation, I know not; but of this I am sure. When her father, with the utmost of his policy and power, sought to

* At this date Smith had published none of his works except his short letter, *A True Relation;* and the extended narratives of the *General History,* afterwards, were by others.

surprise me, having but eighteen with me, the dark night could not affright her from coming through the irksome woods, and with watered eyes gave me intelligence with her best advice to escape his fury; which, had he known, he had surely slain her. (Dost thou remember Anas, on York River, at that night supper?) "

"Yes, I remember," I say in answer.

"Jamestown with her wild train (he continueth reading) she as freely frequented as her father's habitation; and during the time of two or three years she, next under God, was still the instrument to preserve this Colony from death, famine, and utter confusion, which if in those times had once been dissolved, Virginia might have lain as it was at our first arrival to this day."

"That is God's truth!" I say. "You put it in noble words, most worthy Captain."

"Thus, most gracious Lady" (Smith goes on reading), "however this might be presented you from a more worthy pen, it cannot from a more honest heart. As yet I never begged anything of the state or any, and it is my want of ability and her exceeding desert; your birth, means, and authority; her birth, virtue, want, and simplicity, doth make me thus bold humbly to beseech your Majesty to take this knowledge of the Lady Pokahontas; and so I humbly kiss your Majesty's gracious hands and rest."

Therewith Smith rolls up his paper, which he says is copied from what he writ the Queen when the ship with my little Lady comes to Plymouth. I listen to all this, not marvelling at his quick thought of her; and see now, that this letter brings the Queen to knowledge of her, whence all her gracious acts to my Lady and her reception at Court. The man that loved her (Smith) stills his poor beating heart that she is married to another now, and does that he can for the blessed damozel that is gone from him.

Now by this time it was nigh sunset and the courtiers were gone. Smith thinks he will go too, and asks, what good of speech with her? He cannot meet her as in old days when she was little Pokahontas.

"She is now Lady Rebecca," he says, "and one of a royal family. His Majesty calls her cousin, and chides his subject Master Rolfe, I 'm told, for marrying a Princess. Sure to be again familiar to her would hurt her in her new rank, to speak

nothing of her husband, who little fancies *They meet again.*
(I think) old loves!"

These bitter words he says, and heaves a sigh and then is quiet.

"It is best," he says lowly. "What so hard as to thus meet her that once was my sweetheart, and talk coldly to my Lady Rebecca; I that fain would clasp her close and weep on her bosom! So no more, Anas! I will go away. Take thou this paper and show it her."

"Show it her yourself," I say; "here she is."

And indeed my little Lady, grown weary of the Court people and knowing not we were in the garden, walks for rest there and comes out suddenly from the bosk and sees us. Smith rises up quick and stands facing her in a great tremble. She is shaking too and comes on slow toward him, looking at him. Sudden she covers her face with her hands, and I see the tears stealing through her fingers. Smith goes to her and bows low, calling her my Lady Rebecca ; but thereat she cries : —

"No! no! call me not that, but what thou calledst me in Virginia!"

Thereat Smith turns a little white and says in a strange voice : —

"I owe my Lady too much respect. Sure a married woman belongs to her lord, and the King hath forbid you to be treated save as a Princess. Forget the old times and remember the new. It were far better ! "

He speaks deep, well nigh groaning, but she wrings her hands and cries pitifully once more : —

" No ! no ! Thou didst call me ' child ' once. I would be the same still ; and if ' child,' then ' father ! ' Wouldst thou not have that ? You did promise Powhatan what was yours should be his, and he the like to you. You called him ' father,' being in his land a stranger ! "

Thereat a blush comes to her face as though thinking, Were I married to him then my father would be his, and my father's child his wife !

But Smith, drawing a long breath, shakes his head and stands in a sort of quaking.

" The child forgot one who loved her," he says, speaking very low.

And she in a voice yet lower : —

" They did tell me always you were dead, and I knew no other till I came to Plymouth."

Whereat her face grows so white that

I think she will faint; but she stands straight and looks at him out of her great black eyes, that are swimming in tears, as though her heart were breaking.

Sudden I, Anas Todkill, remembering myself, go away from these two people. Lost in amaze I had stood thus far scarce knowing I listened. Now I turn round and slowly leave them, and they walk away each beside other; and then the bosk of the wood taketh them, and they are no more seen.

What said they each to other? I know not nor would know. Sure the secrets of these two hearts were their own, and, as 't were, sacred. After an hour they come back slowly, and I can see my Lady has been weeping. Smith is pale, and his voice shakes as he bows low and goes away; and then my Lady steals to her bower and is no more seen that night. Master Rolfe plays chuck-farthing with a friend, asking "Who's been to-day?" And I go out in the moon that is shining and look up to my Lady's window, and say, "Write me a great drama, O worthy Master Shake-speare! Thou dost sound the human heart — canst thou sound these two?"

XXVIII.

How my Lady Pokahontas passed in Peace.

My Lady would return to Virginia. IT is little I have to add now to this true relation of my Lady Pokahontas. After that last greeting with him she had once loved she fell into a great melancholy ; and save for thoughts of her religion I think she had pined away then, and so ended. But her faith kept her from despairing, and she would talk always of going back to Virginia. Her own people were to be converted, and she would be God's instrument, — wherefore in the very beginning of this poor discourse I writ the words, that the fabric of that great business fell in her grave.

Natheless, always she had it at heart, in that autumn and the winter that followeth ; seeming no more to think of Smith (now made by his Majesty Admiral of New England), but dreameth what she may do, as a poor servant of the Lord Christ.

Oft I hear her whisper "Virginia !" as

one musing in her mind : and once she *But falls asleep.*
toucheth me with her small hand, and rais-
ing her black eyes to my face, saith low,
with faint smiles : "Come thou with me,
Anas !"

Certes, I had gone with her on that voyage they made ready for : but, sudden (as
I said) my little Lady set forth on another.

It fell (so God willed) in the March
month of the year of our blessed Lord
1617, at Gravesend. My Lady had gone
thither to embark for Virginia, carrying
the blessing of his grace the Bishop of
London on her intent in her own country.
But she never was to see the fair fields of
Virginia more. A fever takes her and she
sinks suddenly, but is resigned to God's will,
and blesses his name. I was close to her
when she died, and signing the people to
leave her she whispers to me : —

"You will love my boy, Anas," she says,
in a voice I scarce hear ; "and say to *some
one*, thou knowest who, he must love and
cherish him too for his poor mother."

Thereat she looks up and joins her two
white hands together.

"Blessed Jesus, thou wilt have me !"
she whispers, and comes a sudden still-
ness. My Lady is ended.

She passed in peace.

She lies buried in the chancel of the parish church of Gravesend, there waiting the resurrection, when the secrets of all hearts shall be known. This one was so white that I think no stain be there to wash. But natheless, if there be, Christ's blood will take it away; since whether

a poor maid in Virginia, or a
royal princess in England, my
little Lady trusted in
Him, and passed in
peace.

(Writ by Anas Todkill, Puritan and Pilgrim, sometime her henchman, who commendeth to all good people this True Relation. 1618.)